The Stone Soup Book
of Animal Stories

The Stone Soup Book of ANIMAL Stories

By the Young Writers of Stone Soup Magazine

Edited by
GERRY MANDEL, WILLIAM RUBEL,
and MICHAEL KING

•

Children's Art Foundation
Santa Cruz, California

The Stone Soup Book of Animal Stories
Gerry Mandel, William Rubel, and Michael King, editors

Copyright © 2013 by the Children's Art Foundation

•

Stone Soup Magazine
Children's Art Foundation
P.O. Box 83
Santa Cruz, CA 95063

www.stonesoup.com

•

ISBN: 978-0-89409-026-4

Book design by Jim MacKenzie
Printed in the U.S.A.

Cover illustration by Abigail Stephens, age 12,
for "Badger Will Be Badger," page 63

About Stone Soup

Stone Soup, the international magazine of stories, poems, and art by children, is published six times a year out of Santa Cruz, California. Founded in 1973, *Stone Soup* is known for its high editorial and design standards. The editors receive more than 10,000 submissions a year by children ages 8 to 13. Less than one percent of the work received is published. Every story and poem that appears in *Stone Soup* is remarkable, providing a window into the lives, thoughts, and creativity of children.

Stone Soup has published more writing and art by children than any other publisher. With our anthologies, we present some of the magazine's best stories in a new format, one designed to be enjoyed for a long time. Choose your favorite genre, or collect the whole set.

Contents

Phoebe

by Erin Cadora, age 10

IT WAS A QUAINT little backyard, not much, but cozy, a haven for many strays. With pretty, plump azalea bushes to dash into, and a soft, ivy-covered ground to sleep on, a homeless kitty could spend a few comfortable nights there. Of course, it was never a permanent home of any stray, but there was one who was different.

She was not quite full-grown, but not a kitten either. Her stomach was as white and fluffy as a cloud, but her tail, back, and the top of her head were a thunderstorm gray. She had petite paws and innocent features. Her face consisted of glittering, clever, but frightened eyes and an adorable little pink nose that almost sparkled in the sunlight. She had obviously had a previous home, because there was a silver bell attached to her neck by a red velvet strap. Unfortunately, her previous owner had most likely abused her; she was petrified of humans and always had that anxious look in her eyes.

She had certainly taken quite a shine to that garden, and had

Erin was living in Brooklyn, New York, when her story appeared in the March/April 2008 issue of Stone Soup.

THE STONE SOUP BOOK

seemed to settle there, but she took care not to venture near the crusted old brownstone that towered above her. Little did she know, the woman who lived in that house was interested in her, she was curious about the cat that lived in her yard. She also took pity on the poor thing; she was scared the kitty might starve. Every time the cat tried to sneak up on a bird or squirrel, her bell would jingle, scaring the critter away, and leaving her hungry. She was beginning to grow slim and slightly weak. The woman thought the cat was adorable, but didn't even consider taking her in. She still hadn't gotten over the recent loss of her pet cat that was very dear to her, Robert. He had been a unique cat, playful and mischievous, but all the more lovable. She still wanted to do something for the young kitty, so she decided that she would try to take her bell off. She stepped gingerly into the yard, trying not to make too much noise. But the second the cat caught a glimpse of the woman, she darted behind a tree, not wanting anything to do with people.

The woman was determined to get that cat something to eat, and she had an idea for the next day. When she got home from work, she carelessly tossed her bag aside, eager to help the sweet young cat. She grabbed a paper plate and poured some cat food on it. Again, she stepped outside as gingerly as possible, but the cat sprung into the azaleas. From the fragments of world visible from in between the dense bushes, the cat saw the woman put something down on the ground and walk back into the house. The cat was puzzled. Why would the woman put down a white disc with little brown circles? she thought. Intrigued, she slinked out of her hiding place and over to the unknown object. She sniffed, and a wonderful scent (in her opinion) erupted from the plate. She inhaled deeper and deeper until she was scarfing down the food. She knew the meal was from the woman, and she assumed she was kind, but felt she couldn't trust humans yet; ugly flashes of her old life still remained in her mind.

The woman's interest in the cat had turned to a love for her. She had fed her and watched her in a motherly fashion for a couple weeks, and was almost sure she could welcome the beautiful creature into her home. But sorrowful memories of poor Robert's death still lurked in her mind, and she didn't know if she could handle taking in another cat. As she debated with herself, she practiced her routine of pouring some cat food onto a plate and toptoeing outside.

The cat cleansed her paws with her rough little tongue as she, too, thought about whether or not she would like to live with the woman. After the woman had given her several meals, feelings of affection for her food supplier had grown. She stopped, alert, with her ears perked up as the woman stepped outside to give her food, but she did not run away. The two maintained eye contact right until the minute the woman walked into her home, but didn't close the door. The cat looked at the food, then at the awaiting open door, and listlessly but surely walked into the house.

Thirteen years later, a plump, aged, affectionate cat named Phoebe purrs relentlessly as she nuzzles the sleeping daughter of the woman who took her in.

King of the Forest

by Josepha Natzke, age 13

THE FOREST WAS STILL. The birds had ceased their songs, the squirrels their chattering. Even the wind seemed to hold its breath as the woods prepared for the night. Rabbits had long since crept to their warrens, and mice were scampering to their burrows as owls shook out their wings to go hunt in the night air.

Only one figure was still awake under the trees, standing in a small clearing near the edge of the woods. It was the king of the forest, a magnificent buck, his huge antlers rising like a menacing crown around him as he stood silhouetted against the dying sun, his eyes piercing the gloom of the forest.

What exactly the buck was waiting for, he was not yet sure. Perhaps it was the quietness of the forest this night, or perhaps the instinct that told him that danger was lurking nearby.

A sudden change of the wind confirmed his suspicions, and from the bushes at the edge of the glade he could smell life—living, breathing, hungry life. Cougar.

The buck's mind flew to other parts of the forest, where does

Josepha was living in Newberg, Oregon, when her story appeared in the January/February 2010 issue of Stone Soup.

and fawns lay asleep in the wood, so vulnerable and innocent. Without the buck to protect them they would be helpless, easy prey. Yes, the king was old, but if he did go down it would not be without a fight.

Slowly and cleverly he turned away from the bushes and pretended to graze along the ground, looking for all the world like unsuspecting prey. The trick appeared to work, for with a terrible snarl a huge mountain lion erupted from the bushes, his face distorted as he leaped for his prey. But the king was ready. Easily he sprang aside and the cougar crashed to the ground, where the buck's sharp hooves rained down blows on him. But the cat was hungry. It had not eaten for a while. It would not let go so easily.

Almost too quick to be seen its paw flashed out, knocking the deer's feet out from under him. The buck toppled and the cat leaped up, going for the neck. For a moment it was flailing hooves and claws, a blur of tawny and soft brown fur. But somehow the buck was back on his hooves before the cougar could pin him, and he rammed his great antlers into the cougar's side.

That was enough. Yowling and screaming, the cat scrambled to his feet and fled from the woods, both hungry and beaten, never to be seen again.

The buck stood again at the center of the clearing. Once again, he was victorious. Silently, looking around the glade once more, the king passed into the darkening forest at last.

The sun set.

Shadow

by Katya B. Schwenk, age 11

FOR A FEW DAYS in mid-September, the temperature seems perfect. It's not boiling hot, but it hasn't reached what you would call freezing cold yet. It's a little chilly, but that makes you feel fresh and wide awake, and the wind isn't horribly wild and hasn't started biting at your face.

It was one of those days, and so my dad and I drove down to the local woods to go for a walk.

The ride was short, and I entertained myself by looking at the trees' beautiful gowns of gold, red, and orange. Here and there, a pine tree popped up, looking serious and glum compared to the others around it.

We stopped and parked in the small lot. I got out, and a cool, crisp breeze brushed my cheek and ruffled my blond hair.

We started walking, and our feet crunched on the forest floor. Sometimes—in a sudden gust of wind—a brightly colored leaf would float gently down, adding to the great carpet of foliage already resting there.

Katya was living in South Burlington, Vermont, when her story appeared in the September/October 2009 issue of Stone Soup.

We talked some, but I usually skipped ahead of my dad, my hair whipping back, and breathed in the fresh, earthy smell of the forest.

After a ways, about thirty minutes after we started, a bubbling stream wound itself towards us and continued to race merrily along the path.

As we rounded a bend, I noticed a skinny, black animal drinking from the stream. I froze, for my first thought was, bear.

My dad didn't notice it at first but then stopped as well.

He was a black Lab that was obviously lost—or a stray. His fur was matted, and his ribs were showing. But there was also something around his neck. It wasn't a collar—I could tell that much—but more like a piece of string.

The animal heard our footsteps and turned to look at us.

Well, he seemed to be looking at *me*.

He wasn't just *looking*, however. He was almost talking to me in a way I couldn't explain—the way animals seem to give messages to humans without words, through just their eyes. This dog's eyes were like melted chocolate, and if I had to say what he was conveying to me in words, it would be, "Help me."

Still frozen, I peered closely at him, trying to see what the thing around his neck was. But instead, I found myself gazing back into those eyes, as if I could not look away.

And then the dog came slowly, tentatively, towards us, his tail wagging slowly.

My dad unfroze and walked toward the dog, just as slowly as the dog walked toward him. Then my dad said, "Hannah, let's get the dog back to the car, OK? Then we'll take him to the Humane Society—he obviously needs help."

Unfreezing, I nodded. "Come on," I coaxed.

The dog was too willing. He bounded towards us, then stopped, and limped the rest of the way; his leg was hurt, it seemed.

Half an hour later, we were in the small parking lot, and my dad was looking at the map to find the route to the Humane

THE STONE SOUP BOOK

Society. I was looking at the thing around the dog's neck. Tied on a red string was a piece of paper.

In small, messy handwriting it said, "Please take care of Shadow."

Immediately, my heart went out to the dog. How could someone do that? How could someone let a dog survive on his or her own? And then a small question formed in my mind. What would have happened to Shadow if we hadn't found him?

Trying not to think about the answer to that question, I paid more attention to Shadow. His fur was as black as a raven, and one of his ears had a chunk missing from it. On the way back, I had petted him, but my dad said something about ticks, and so I stopped.

But he had to agree with me that this dog was very cute. Well, if he was a little bit plumper, and his fur was brushed, he'd be adorable.

When my dad folded the map and put it away, I dared to ask him, "Dad, can we keep Shadow?"

"Shadow?" he asked. Then he sighed. "Hannah honey, you've named the dog already? You know we can't keep him."

"No, look, Dad, it says on his tag."

"He has a collar?"

"No, look."

My dad crouched down and looked at the tag that had been around his neck. I could see his lips forming the words as he read them.

Again, he sighed. "Well, let's get going, Hannah."

I nodded, looking at Shadow. He was pacing around us, glancing sadly at me with his big brown eyes.

We got in the car, and Shadow sat in the back, panting happily.

"Can we keep him, Dad?" I pleaded.

"No, Hannah," my dad said firmly. "We can't. I'm sorry."

"Please, please, please?" I begged.

"Sorry, Hannah," said my dad.

"I just don't want him to go to someone who'll abandon him

again," I said.

My dad sighed. "There are other people who care about dogs, sweetie," said my dad.

"I know," I said. "But what if he gets placed in a home that doesn't care?"

"He won't," said my dad. "That's what the Humane Society is careful about."

I turned my attention to the trees again, but somehow they didn't seem so interesting anymore.

Half an hour later, we arrived at the building. We walked inside and I found myself in a room that had cages with cats in them, guinea pigs chattering anxiously, and sounds of barking dogs echoing through it. I wanted to take each cat home, and each gerbil and hamster as well. The lady took Shadow, and my dad dragged me out of the Humane Society.

Though I begged my parents for Shadow, they refused. I pouted. They wouldn't give in.

Finally, *I* had to give in, which was something I knew was going to happen all along. But it wasn't because of my parents' stubbornness; it was because Shadow was adopted.

For about three weeks, my heart leaped whenever I saw a black Lab. I strained to see if it might have been Shadow. But none of them were quite right—maybe too small or too big. Or when I asked to pet them, they didn't recognize me or look at me in the way Shadow did.

But Shadow might not recognize you, Hannah, I thought. He barely even knew you. I knew it was true, but I couldn't make myself believe it.

Once a month of that passed, I gave up. I just hoped that Shadow had been adopted into a good home and put it out of my mind. I had just entered middle school and was thinking about other things.

A year passed. My dad and I were walking down the street on a fall afternoon one day. The trees reminded me of the ones that were so beautiful on the day I first met Shadow. Suddenly,

I saw out of the corner of my eye an eight-year-old boy and his mother walking down the street with their dog, a plump black Lab. I turned my head. There was something about this dog that I couldn't quite place. The Lab had a red collar on, and one of his ears had a piece missing. He trotted happily beside the two and was looked at in adoration by the boy. As I passed them, the dog turned his head towards me and almost said something to me with eyes like melted chocolate, which were carefree and untroubled. He said (if I had to translate), "I'll be OK." Then he turned his head back to the boy and his mother and continued his walk.

I stood there, glued to the pavement, watching them head down the street until they disappeared. "Hannah, c'mon," said my dad. Silently, I turned away from the empty sidewalk and followed him, feeling complete; the worry that Shadow would be mistreated or neglected seemed to have vanished into thin air.

Now I have a gray kitten with a white blotch around one eye. Her name is Lark, and she looks at me with bright blue eyes that are like rivers and almost talks to me in the way Shadow did—the way all animals can do.

Flying Against the Wind

by *Christopher Fifty, age 13*

I N A MARSH, long green grass reaching up to touch the sun swayed slightly in the cool morning breeze. The marsh was teeming with animal and insect life. A snake slithered through the grasses looking for mice while an osprey swooped low overhead, wind ruffling its feathers. The osprey was looking for an animal to catch; a fish was on the main course for today. He needed to find a big fish or several smaller fish to feed his mate and chicks. He headed towards the river, wind pushing him forward like an arrow shot from a bow.

The osprey was happy; he was always happy just flying, hunting, sleeping, and mating. A powerful hawk, he didn't need to worry about being the prey to some bigger animal. His chicks, on the other hand, did. Eagles were known to come flying by and snatch hatchlings to eat. The osprey promised himself that he would never let that happen to his chicks. He loved his chicks, and would easily sacrifice his life for theirs, and so would his mate. She would fly out of their nest and peck and claw an invader until

Christopher was living in Churchville, Maryland, when his story appeared in the March/April 2010 issue of Stone Soup.

THE STONE SOUP BOOK

he retreated, defeated. Ground animals couldn't get to their nest because the tree they picked was about twenty-three feet high and had sharp branches jutting out from the base. His mate always stayed with their chicks. Often when he came home he would see their chicks huddled under her warm fluffy wings.

He finally arrived at the river. It was fast moving and clear. He felt the thrill of excitement he always felt when he was going hunting. He was going to catch a big fish worthy of his wife and three chicks. He swooped into a dive. He loved the sensation of the wind rushing past his head. He pulled out of it about three feet from the surface of the water, looked quickly for a fish, and then swooped in. He dove quickly and made a splash as his talons entered the water. The fish, alarmed by the commotion from the ripples, tried to get away. Too late. The osprey speared the fish with his talons, piercing through the scales and deep into the flesh. He quickly flew up, the fish's head dangling in the air.

With a tight grip, he headed to his nest where his chicks would be with his mate. He was flying against the wind, which made it harder, but he prevailed. He finally reached his nest. He saw his mate, with their chicks under her wings, and felt happy that he had such a good family. That night they ate well.

Memory's Song

by Mary Woods, age 11

WE SHOULD HAVE known better," Garu grated angrily. The sparrow perched high in the apple tree, watching helplessly as the gray cat below devoured her kill. "Let's leave. This is no place for the clan." His fierce gaze flicked over his now small group: his trusted friend Baklan, Baklan's mate Teekeh, their grown daughter Kila, and his own son, Liru.

Liru looked up to him with imploring eyes. "Where? Where is there?"

The sharpness in Garu's voice changed to weariness. "I don't know. But someplace."

He took off and the group followed suit. The summer evening air was cool and refreshing, but Garu could not enjoy it. He tried to keep his eyes ahead, but they kept glancing backwards at his son. Why did Liru have to have those pale brown feathers like his mother? Why did he have to serve as a reminder of that terrible event? A pain slashed through his heart. He remembered it all too well.

Mary was living in Frankfort, Illinois, when her story appeared in the September/October 2009 issue of Stone Soup.

THE STONE SOUP BOOK

H E AND LIRANA were flying together on a summer evening. The breeze was sweet and the sunset was radiant. It turned the green leaves of the forest below to gold. Little pink clouds skipped across the colorful horizon. He could see the smile on Lirana's face and the gentle sparkle in her eye; a smile of pride at bringing up her first child. Their son Liru was a few weeks old and needed plenty of care, but Teekeh had offered to watch him for a while. Garu and his mate had eagerly taken the opportunity to enjoy the sunset and soar in the pleasant sky. And as Lirana let out a laugh of happiness and did a loop-the-loop in the air, Garu felt as if there was nothing more he could possibly want.

A screech rang in the quiet air, and suddenly all was chaos.

Lirana screamed as the owl swooped towards her. The great talons were wide open, waiting to snatch prey out of the air. They closed with a snap—but Lirana was quicker. Her little pale brown wings tilted ever so slightly and escaped the flying predator. This happened once, twice, three times, and still the sparrow evaded the owl with inches to spare. But it could not last much longer.

Meanwhile, Garu sat stupidly watching the scene from a branch he had crashed into when he had dived to avoid the owl. He yearned to help, but he was overpowered by fear. He was frozen in place.

It had been growing steadily darker. The owl's eyes were accustomed to the night, but Lirana's were not. She was constantly twisting and turning. Then suddenly, in her inability to see, she doubled back—straight into the owl's claws.

Her scream rent the air, and then all was silent as the predator flew away with his kill.

Garu felt numb all over. His claws came loose, and he fell from the branch. He landed in a soft pile of leaves, where he wept uncontrollably.

A FTER THAT, he had left the forest, unable to stay at the place of his mate's death. He had moved from one place to another—swamps, farms, cities, prairies, but never forests. He could not bear to be reminded. But everywhere he went, at least part of the clan was killed by one thing or another. And whenever they were, he left again, searching for a safer territory. But nothing had improved. Predators had picked off the clan one by one, until their number was reduced to a mere five.

Suddenly, a screech rang in the quiet air, and instantly all was chaos.

"Dad! Heeelp!!"

Garu's head whipped around at the sound of his son's cry. A huge mottled owl was diving towards him, and Liru was flapping desperately. Garu's heart skipped a beat, and then it plummeted down to his stomach. The nightmare was happening all over again.

Baklan, Teekeh, and Kila had fled towards the fields below, leaving Liru to his fate. But Garu refused to do the same. This time he would not sit dumbly watching his loved one die. He forced his wings to beat, and darted through the air towards his son. "I'm coming, Liru!"

It seemed as if Garu had gone back into time. There was the little pale brown streaked sparrow, dodging and ducking, twisting and spinning. And there was the huge bird of prey, swooping and grasping thin air with gleaming talons. But this time Garu was not a spectator. He was a pursuer.

Suddenly, he slammed into the owl's back, and as soon as he realized what he had run into, he began tearing the owl's feathers out, ripping and scratching. The owl was surprised at this ambush and rapidly dived down. Garu fell off the predator's back and fell. But just in time he opened his wings and swooped upwards. He spotted his son flying away to safety and followed him into the darkness.

The clack of claws sounded next to his ear, and there was a rush of air, ruffling his gray-brown feathers.

The owl was after him.

As he spun away to one side and then to the next, he saw Liru heading towards him. Regardless of his own safety, Liru was returning to help his father.

"Liru, go!" screamed Garu. "Go, now!" He felt the whiff of air and tilted his wings to avoid the keen claws.

"No!" his son shouted back. "I'm not going anywhere!" And he flew ever closer.

"Liru, don't you dare..." He never finished. Something sharp tore at his shoulder, and then he was free-falling, his wing flapping painfully and uselessly. The last thing he saw before he blacked out was the illuminated golden eyes of the owl, and beyond that, his son hovering in the dark sky.

L ONG INTO the starry night Baklan watched for Garu's return. He and Teekeh and Kila had flown down to a dense thicket when the owl had attacked. But Garu had stayed and tried to save his son. But Baklan knew that Liru would never return. He figured it would be just the same as every time. Garu would come back with hard eyes and a hardened heart. And now that his son had been killed here, he would probably avoid the open country as well as forests. And they would move on and on.

Garu did not return that night. The three sparrows waited all through the next morning and afternoon, and finally when the sun began to set, he appeared on the horizon. Even from this distance, Baklan could tell that his wing-beats were heavy.

Baklan took off from the thornbush and flew out to meet his leader. But as he approached, he saw that there was something wrong. Garu's feathers were of a darker hue than this sparrow's. And this bird was smaller and slimmer... no... it couldn't be...

It was Liru.

Baklan's steady flight faltered as he recognized Garu's son. "Liru! You were... how did... where... Liru, you're alive!"

"I'd rather not be." The young sparrow brushed past Baklan and alighted wearily in the thicket. Puzzled, Baklan turned around and followed.

He found Liru staring towards the north, towards their forest home. Baklan fluttered over next to him. Liru did not turn to look at the older sparrow, but his next words were addressed to him. "My father would have wanted me to lead the clan. In honor of his death, I will accept the position. We will leave for the forest at dawn." There was something of Garu in the determined way he said these words.

"Yes, sir," Baklan nodded smartly. "Should I take a night watch?"

"No. That is my duty. I wouldn't be able to sleep anyways."

"Yes, sir." He crept down to a lower branch and settled down comfortably. And he peered at Liru's silhouette until the last rays of the sun disappeared on the horizon, and he fell asleep.

G ARU AWOKE coughing and spluttering, water pouring out of his mouth. He was drenched to the bone. His shoulder ached unbearably. Only when he was finished coughing up water did he hear the gentle voice. "That's right. Feel better now? You surprised me; I never saw a sparrow in a stream before. And a good thing I got you out too; you were nearly drowned."

Garu stumbled on unsteady legs and painfully turned around. There, smiling in a friendly way at him, was a dark brown water rat. "Who... who are you?" But his speech came out in a whisper, and it set off another bout of coughing.

"That's all right, you don't have to talk. I'm Hrimi. This is my den. I saw you floating in the stream nearby and dragged you out. I didn't know if you were dead or unconscious, but I took you in anyway. And here you are, well and alive."

"Alive," Garu agreed in a low voice, "but not well." He shifted his position slightly and winced as pain shot through his wing.

"Yes, we'll have to do something about that shoulder. Wait here, I think I've got just the right herb in my storerooms." Hrimi scurried off.

Garu took the time to observe his surroundings. He was sitting in a warm, dry burrow in the ground. The burrow must have been deep because the ceiling was high and arched. Roots

THE STONE SOUP BOOK

lined the roof; there must have been a tree growing above him. The room was large and airy. Three windows at the top illuminated the space and the sunlight shining in made it cheerful. Dried grasses lined the hole, and there were a couple of tunnels leading to the rat's storage rooms. Hrimi looked old. He couldn't have dug this all by himself.

The hospitable water rat came back with a few dried leaves and a mortar and pestle. "You need to drink this, so I'm crushing it up," he explained.

As the water rat ground the herb, Garu looked around at the room in marvel. "Did you dig this?" he inquired.

"Oh, no!" Hrimi laughed. "My father and my brothers did. I was the youngest. They're all dead and gone now. But we had good times. Yes, we did. I remember my father teaching me how to swim. He was proud of me, the way I caught on quicker than my older brothers had." The rat sighed happily at the memory. "Those were good days. I miss them, and sometimes I feel real lonely, but then I remember one of those happy times and I'm all right again. I'm contented. I'm glad I live in the burrow my father dug."

And Garu pondered over what he said.

LIRU WATCHED the snow fall gently past him. Last summer he had led the clan back to the forest where he had been born. There Baklan had recognized a few friends of his, and these had willingly joined the group. Their number had gradually grown to around twenty sparrows, and Liru led them. He was happy with his life, except for one thing. The thought of his father had always bothered him. He had never found out whether or not Garu had really died. On that far-off summer day he had searched all along the place where his father fell, but not a trace of him could he find. He assumed Garu was dead, and he forced himself to accept it. But still there was a tiny glimmer of hope, like a flickering candle on a stormy, starless night, that refused to be put out.

Liru gazed upon the clan of sparrows chatting and laughing below. Liru wished he could join in their happiness. But this winter day had reminded him of another long ago, when the ever-shrinking clan, under Garu, had moved to a swamp. The wind was bitter, and it rattled and shrieked in the cattails like a great predator. Liru had been frightened on that frigid winter dawn. Then suddenly he had spotted his father above him, perching in the reeds, watching over his family. And Liru was reassured.

Now, he glanced up as he had long ago. His eyes narrowed. That bump on that limb above him hadn't been there before. He tried to focus in on it, but the white flakes falling past made it difficult. And then—it *moved.*

At the same time that warning flags went up in Liru's head, the tiny glimmer of hope that his father would return began to grow out of control. It flared up and licked at the doubtful part of him, burning it up into nothing but a smoldering memory. Then it blazed brighter and brighter, until hope gleamed in his eyes and he cried out, "Father!"

The figure took off from the limb and dived towards him. Liru spread his wings as well, and time seemed to slow down to a crawl.

A sparrow was floating towards him through the snowy air. His eyes were bright and eager, and his feathers were shining with health. There was pride in those eyes. Pride for his son.

Liru's heart leaped up into his throat with joy. He linked his claws with those of Garu, and they spun round and round together until their wings could beat no more; then they tumbled down, breathless and dizzy, into the soft white snow. They stared at each other for a moment, breathing hard. But when Liru opened his mouth to speak, Garu shook his head.

"No need to say sorry, Liru. It wasn't your fault, so don't blame yourself. I'm here and I want to know all your adventures."

As they flew up to a branch overlooking the clan, Liru explained all that had happened, and how he had been confused about Garu. "But now," he concluded, "I'm so happy I could sing."

"Do so," Garu grinned, and his son obeyed.

A song came pouring forth from the depth of Liru's heart, bubbling and spilling over like a waterfall of notes. It flowed and chuckled like a stream, then changed to long, sweet tones, savored and heartfelt. Then finally it ended triumphant and strong, like trumpets after a battle is won.

Garu spoke quietly in a dreamy, far-away voice. "You sound just like your mother did."

"Really?" Liru asked, pleased.

"Oh, yes. Did you know that was how I met her? Her voice echoed sweet and strong throughout the whole forest. All the males flocked around her, hoping she would pick one of them for a mate. She used to sing you to sleep when you were frightened of the night and its noises. Do you remember that?"

"Yes, I do," Liru nodded. He paused for a moment, then said hesitantly, "You... you seem happy to talk about her."

"I am," Garu confirmed. "Yes, she was a wonderful sparrow. I'm *glad* to have known her. I'm glad to be back."

From Terror to Triumph

by Bailey Bergmann, age 12

A LOW GROWL vibrated out of his snarling jaws. Drool trickled over the cruelly glinting teeth and onto the cracked concrete sidewalk where he stood in a threatening stance. His brown eyes, which portrayed nothing but pure hatred, pierced the small toddler's who stood stiff with fear in front of him. The little girl, four years old at the time, was frozen in a trance, too afraid to run, or even tremble. A scream was caught in the back of her throat that would not escape. A lower growl from her assailer at last set it free.

"Mommy!" the girl shrieked. The dog pounced with a sickening half-growl and half-yelp, and all Asa remembered was hitting the concrete with the dog's hot breath on her neck.

M Y FAVORITE ANIMAL has to be dogs."

"Hmm?" Asa was jerked out of that nightmarish recollection as she realized her friend Jenny was talking to her.

"Hello?" Jenny joked. "Anybody home in there?"

Bailey was living in Shawano, Wisconsin, when her story appeared in the September/October 2007 issue of Stone Soup.

"Sorry," Asa replied, shifting her crystal-blue backpack to her left shoulder. "I was just thinking."

"About what?"

Asa shrugged. Not many people knew about the incident of her and the aggressive dog, even though it had been all over the news when it had happened. Asa rubbed her throat gently, running her finger along the familiar five-inch-long scar that ran along the side of her neck, curving into the middle of her throat. Jenny, like most people who knew Asa, had in the past asked where she got the scar, but Asa always replied evasively, "In an accident." So far, she hadn't met anyone who had pushed to know the full story.

"Well, you have to see my neighbor's new puppies," Jenny went on with her dialogue. "There are three of them, two boys and a girl, and they are just the *cutest* things in this world."

"What?" Asa interrupted, totally lost in the conversation.

"Weren't you listening to me previously?" Jenny chided playfully. "I was talking about Ella's three puppies."

Asa shuddered slightly at the thought of the huge Great Dane. "Ella's Mrs. Lander's dog, right?"

"Yup, and the puppies look just like her." Jenny gave a little skip. "They're just not as big."

Yet, thought Asa. Ella was a sweet, gentle giant, but her size intimidated Asa immensely. And the thought of three more giants like her... Asa shuddered again.

"Are you all right?" Jenny queried, looking into her friend's face. "You look pale."

"Oh no, I'm fine." Asa straightened and smiled, but it was rather strained and unnatural. Jenny looked unconvinced, but she didn't pressure Asa into telling.

"So, do you want to come see Ella's pups with me?" Jenny continued. "Mrs. Lander is letting me come over today, and..."

"No!" Asa almost shouted, with a slight tremble in her voice. Jenny's mouth fell open. Asa blushed and shuffled her feet more quickly. She was almost home. Just around this corner here...

"I better go, Asa," Jenny murmured with a half-confused, half-apologetic glance. "See you."

"Bye, Jenny," Asa sighed with a slight wave of her hand. When her friend had left her, Asa dashed down the sidewalk to her house, as if a mad dog was right at her heels. The door slammed behind her as she jumped through it and skidded into the kitchen, taking a deep breath as she came to a halt. The smell of homemade oatmeal-raisin cookies greeted her like a warm hug, snug and assuring. Asa dropped her backpack and kicked off her new dress shoes that were required for the school's dress code. Asa followed the delicious smell to the oven, where the oven light illuminated two pans of yummy goodness.

BEEP! BEEP! BEEEEP! Asa jumped as the timer blared its warning, and the clatter of footsteps was heard on the stairs. Asa's eighteen-year-old sister, Ann, hurried into the kitchen, snatched an oven mitt, opened the oven door, took out pan number one, set it on the counter, and said, "Hi, Asa," all in one whirl of activity.

After Ann took out the second pan, she asked, "Could you get out the cooling racks, Ace?"

Asa rummaged through a cluttered cabinet and found the racks. She set them on the counter. "Ann?"

"Yes?" Ann thrust a spatula underneath one lightly toasted cookie, and then let it slide off onto a rack with a helping shake.

"Do you think that people should follow all that advice about facing their fears?"

"Well, I guess," Ann replied. "I mean, people can't just live in fear all their lives."

"But what if the fear is something minor?" Asa touched her scar briefly. "Something that won't affect your life very much?"

Ann crossed her arms and leaned against the counter, thinking. "All fear affects your life, Asa." She peered knowingly into Asa's face. "Are you thinking of dogs?"

Asa nodded, taking a warm cookie and gazing at it steadily. "I just—well, I hate being afraid," Asa admitted, breaking the cookie in two and watching the crumbs bounce on the tiled floor and skitter under cabinets. "It's like I'm a wimp, or something. I know most dogs won't hurt me, but I don't believe it."

Ann leaned over and pulled Asa to her side, her shiny black curls touching Asa's light brown forehead.

"Did something happen at school that scared you, Ace?"

Asa shook her head. "All that happened was Jenny invited me to go see three puppies, and I freaked out." Asa sighed. "I think puppies are adorable, but they scare me to death."

Ann's brown eyes shone with understanding. "So what are you going to do about it?"

"What?"

"Are you going to be afraid, or are you going to face your fear?"

Asa was silent, fidgeting with the broken cookie in her hands. At last she looked up. "I think I need the phone."

"ISN'T HE CUTE?" Jenny held a floppy-eared puppy in her arms. His little pink tongue hung out of his mouth in a friendly smile, but Asa still couldn't stop herself from gulping. His teeth looked pretty sharp for a little guy like him.

"Wanna hold him?" Jenny offered, nuzzling the small black-and-white Great Dane. "He's the cutest of the three."

Asa hung back slightly. "Are you sure he won't, um, you know, bite me?"

Jenny laughed. "The closest thing to a bite this baby can manage is a slobbery kiss."

"Are you sure?" Asa said warily. "I've heard puppies sometimes bite."

"They do, but it only feels like little pinpricks when they're babies like him," Jenny responded intelligently. "But he shouldn't do it. He's a pretty mellow fellow." She giggled at her own joke before asking again, "Want to hold him? We could sit down so he's not as wiggly."

"OK," Asa stammered, lowering herself onto the green grass

in the enclosed yard. She eyed Ella lying several feet from her, basking in the sun. Ella's two other puppies were chasing a small white butterfly, having already lost interest in the two visitors.

Asa held out her hands and Jenny eased the chubby puppy from her arms to Asa's. Asa shivered, recollecting that warmth that had caused her pain early on in her childhood. Asa was rigid and nervous, but the puppy in her arms didn't seem to notice. He laid his head lazily on her tense arm, a sigh heaving his chubby middle up. A flicker of a smile crossed Asa's face, and Jenny's grin grew wider.

"Like him?" said Jenny, her head cocked to the side a bit, and her blue eyes shining from behind her lilac-rimmed glasses.

Asa didn't reply for a moment, then she giggled slightly. "Is he hiccupping?"

"He sure is," snickered Jenny. "He hiccups a lot."

Asa used her free arm to timidly stroke the puppy's back, but she steered clear of his mouth. The puppy turned his head towards her hand and Asa gasped as his little mouth lipped her fingers playfully. Asa felt the pinpricks, and shrieked. She scrambled to her feet, the puppy flopping to the ground in Asa's haste.

Jenny hopped up, too, and touched the hand that Asa was clutching. "What's wrong? Are you bleeding?"

"No, no," Asa blurted, pulling away. Tears welled up in her brown eyes, and she turned them downcast. "Look, Jenny, I've gotta go. Can you tell Mrs. Lander thanks for me?"

"Well sure, Asa, but are you sure you're all right?"

"Oh, yes, sure, I'm fine," Asa replied, proving the complete opposite.

For the second time that day, Asa dashed away from her invisible enemy.

"OOH."

Asa glanced up from her bowl of Cheerios to look at Ann. "What?"

"Doesn't a Mrs. Lander live on the next block from here?"

Ann asked, scanning the article in the newspaper she was reading.

Asa's eyes squinted in puzzlement. "Yes. Why do you ask?"

"She was in a car accident yesterday," Ann replied, eyebrows furrowed in sympathy.

"Let me see that, Ann," said their mother, taking the newspaper from her daughter. She glanced over the whole article briefly while Asa squirmed impatiently in her chair.

"What happened, Mom? Is she hurt bad?" Asa tried to look over her mother's shoulder, but she could only see the boldfaced headline: "Woman injured in two-car crash." Asa gulped.

"It says that Mrs. Lander was taking her dog and her three puppies to a veterinarian's appointment yesterday," her mother said, "when a driver shot through a red light and hit Mrs. Lander's car. The other driver wasn't hurt, but Mrs. Lander suffered a broken collarbone and other minor injuries and is now being treated in the hospital."

The three were quiet for a while, Asa more so. She stared intensely into her cereal, as if it would somehow make the whole terrible incident disappear. If Mrs. Lander was hurt in the crash, what about Ella and her puppies?

"Did it say what happened to the dogs?" Asa inquired.

Ann looked over and reported, "'The mother dog and two of her puppies died on the scene. The third was taken to the nearest veterinary clinic.'"

The third, Asa thought. But which one *was* the third?

"JENNY! JENNY!" Asa wove through the crowd of teenagers gathered at her private school's lockers, waving wildly at her friend, who was a little ways ahead. Jenny turned, her face a little ashen.

"Asa!"

Asa stopped to catch her breath. "Did you see the paper this morning?"

"Yeah." Jenny looked down at the floor, her brown shoe tracing a blue speckled tile. "Tragic, isn't it?"

"But which one?" Asa blurted, knowing Jenny would understand what she was talking about. "It wasn't that black-and-white one that I held yesterday, was it?"

Jenny shook her head. "I called all the vets around town, and finally found the one that had Ella's puppy. It's the same one. He's all right, thank goodness, just a little shaken up."

"But his mom!" Asa was now all worked up despite her dreaded phobia. "Won't he starve without her?"

Jenny sighed. "I asked the vet there, and he said that they're bottle-feeding him now." She sighed again. "He also said Mrs. Lander has decided to put the puppy up for adoption."

"But why?"

Jenny shrugged. "My guess is she won't be able to get up and feed him all the times he needs. And besides, she's in the hospital right now with a broken collarbone."

Asa saw how much her friend cared about the puppy. "Don't you want to adopt him?"

Jenny nodded, and said, "But I already have my two rabbits and a cat. Three's the limit, so Mom says." Her blue eyes bore into Asa. "But you don't have any pets."

Asa blinked, trying to comprehend what Jenny was saying. Then it hit her. "You want *me* to adopt him?"

Jenny didn't say anything, but she just stared at Asa, waiting to see what she thought.

Are you going to be afraid, or are you going to face your fear? Ann's words flashed into Asa's memory, as vivid and haunting as the day she was attacked. *People can't just live in fear all their lives... All fear affects your life, Asa.* Asa squeezed her eyes shut, took a deep breath, and then opened them.

"I'll ask, Jenny."

ASA LAY on her stomach, watching Hiccups growl at her fingers that danced in front of him. He snatched her hand in his mouth, but Asa only winced as she gently disentangled herself from his grip. Hiccups' tongue lolled out, and he rolled over onto his back for a belly rub, his tail thwacking the floor and his eyes innocent. Asa giggled, and rubbed the puppy's tummy, making him wiggle all over. As the back door opened, Hiccups flipped onto his stomach, staring at Jenny as she walked in. She held her arms wide, and Hiccups shot into them. Asa smiled. Fear. It does affect your life. But so does joy.

Hiccups tumbled back into her arms for the remainder of his belly rub.

Yes, Asa grinned. *So does joy.*

Half an Eggshell

by Claudia Ross, age 13

I JUMP DOWN the small drop to the grassy road. Tall, brown grass overruns it, thorny weeds branching up from the dry ground. Long stalks of fennel huddle together.

Lizards skitter away from my shoes, and they dart down deep cracks in the earth. The road snakes down the valley. Behind it is a golden brown bluff. Tall grass stands, waving gently—the whole bluff looks like a giant river, swaying back and forth, back and forth.

I run down the hill, summer liberties rising through my stomach. Four days ago I'd graduated from elementary to middle school. The jump was a big one. I was leaving the place that was familiar, that hadn't changed for seven years. The old was comfortable, the new was...

Spiny weeds latch themselves onto my jeans. A noise in the bushes, a hawk calls. They fly by. I slow, reaching a fork in the road. The left fork winds around the back side of the bluff, the right climbs up it.

Claudia was living in Studio City, California, when her story appeared in the May/June 2009 issue of Stone Soup.

I choose left.

Avocado trees hang loose over the trail, casting blotchy late-afternoon shadows. A hawk calls again, flying directly overhead before it lands on a branch. It eyes me, wondering who this stranger is in the middle of his territory. The hawk ruffles its feathers, turning away.

I step back.

Walking slower, I hear only the *swish, swish* of wind through the grass. Another hawk joins the first, but I don't look back. They call to each other, and fly to a closer branch.

Screeeeeee!

Scree-scree-scree-ssscreeee!

Scree-scree screeeeeech!

Their tones are angry—fast and sharp.

Crisp leaves crunch beneath me. Spiny leaves stick to my socks. The trail is winding away from the couple of hawks, up a slight hill. The lizards are still.

A flash of white catches my eye. I bend down, picking up half of an eggshell. It's small; I almost crush it in my hand. The jagged edge is cracked cleanly, where the small bird must have picked his way out. Maybe flew out of the nest. Maybe left his family. Maybe the little bird wasn't ready to go at all...

The trail fades, golden grass taking over. I sit on a low branch, looking through the leaves over the valley. I hear a rustle behind me, looking to see the hawks hopping across the place I've just left. The egg cracks in my grip, pieces of shell fall to the ground.

One of the hawks picks up a leaf in his beak, and it hits me. *They're looking for the egg.* The hawks' calls are more frantic, and they hop back and forth across the mound of leaves where the egg was. I swing my legs around the tree, jumping down. I step softly, quickly, towards the hawks. They back off to the side, flapping onto a branch. I set the eggshell down, then sprint away from the birds, down the hill, through the shadows. I don't hear the hawks until I'm nearly halfway down the road:

Ssssscreeee...

Their tones are gentle—slow and soft.

Sssssscreeeee...

Sssssscreeeeee...

Zitza

by Alexandria Lenzi, age 13

ZAMBIA SAT in a rare patch of green grass, surrounded by
the tall yellow straw-like plants that made up the African savan-
na, her homeland.

This was her place. She came here to be alone with her
thoughts and escape life's anxieties. A feeling of peacefulness
washed over her every time she lay down there. She'd lose herself
in the warm breeze rustling the golden stalks around, welcoming
the feel of the soft grass on her callused feet.

But nothing could cure her sorrow now. A tear slid down
Zambia's dark cheek and landed in the dirt, disappearing almost
immediately as the thirsty ground drank it. She was reminded of
how much she wanted water, and how long she'd been waiting
for some.

Zambia thought she'd lived about fourteen Dry Seasons,
though she didn't know for sure. Dry Season seemed to be getting longer and longer lately. This season had been especially
arid, and water and food were scarce.

*Alexandria was living in Stockton, California, when her story
appeared in the November/December 2008 issue of* Stone Soup.

The water had sunk into the ground and the plants had shriveled up, killing or driving off all the animals. All but one that is.

Zitza had stayed. Zambia had befriended the zebra when they were both young, long before the drought and the sorrow it'd brought. Zitza was the only one who accompanied Zambia to the soft grass.

The zebra dropped her striped head down to Zambia's, nuzzling her cheek. Zambia reached up and entwined her fingers in Zitza's mane, closing her eyes and wishing for rain. Sometimes it seemed like Zitza had the spirit of a girl, not a zebra.

Zambia and her tribe were starving, and many had died from lack of food and water. Many were dying now, including her mother. There was nothing she could do about it. Just wish for rain, rain, rain.

She stood and hoisted herself up onto Zitza's back, wrapping her arms around her friend's neck. A gentle nudge with her foot signaled Zitza to start walking.

She knew where to go. They started off at a trot, breaking into a canter towards home. Running her hands over Zitza's back, Zambia recalled what her father would say about them.

"Zambia's as close to Zitza as Zitza's black stripes are to the white ones," he'd say.

A smile played briefly across her face but vanished as quickly as it'd come. Her father wasn't like that anymore—not since the drought.

They reached the small village they lived in. It was mostly mud and thatch huts with a little altar and figurine at the center.

Zambia's family hut was the farthest away from the others—and the closest to the Bush. When they arrived, she slid off Zitza's back and led her to her arena, which she'd made years ago for the zebra.

"Good night, dear Zitza," she whispered, and went inside.

Her father greeted her solemnly and said good night. Zambia knelt by her mother, who was lying down already, her eyes closed. It hurt Zambia to see her so thin and her stomach bloated with deprivation of water.

After kissing her hot forehead, Zambia retreated to the opposite side of the hut and prepared herself for sleep. She closed her eyes and dreamed of cool, clear water raining down out of the heavens.

ZAMBIA AWOKE to her father gently shaking her by the shoulders.

"Wake up, Zambia!" he said, his voice hushed so as to not wake her mother. "I need you to go look for insects to eat."

"But father," she answered dazedly, "no one's been able to find any."

"*Please*, Zambia." He looked into her eyes, his own filled with sorrow. She knew he needed her to leave. Was it something to do with her mother?

"*Please.*"

She nodded and got up reluctantly. Her father hugged her, to her surprise, and Zambia could see tears in his eyes. *What was going on?*

"Go," he said, not unkindly, and gave her a push towards the door.

Confused, Zambia walked out, past the arena, and into the rough golden sea of tall grass. She thought about bringing Zitza, but when she looked back at her, she decided to let her rest. The zebra had been sleeping against the fence, reminding Zambia of her starving mother who was still asleep.

Looking for insects was a very hard task, seeing as there weren't any to find. But the thought of locust cooked over an open fire, its scent traveling on the breeze, its crunchy outside giving way to her teeth, kept her going. It had been so long since she'd eaten.

Zambia finally decided to give up, for it was already midday, and she couldn't find anything. She didn't want to disappoint her father, but the task he'd given her was impossible.

She walked into the village at the opposite side of where her hut was. She passed many homes, a few with owners no longer living. Zambia had almost reached her home when she saw it.

A zebra skin was stretched across the ground.

Zambia's stomach lurched. She stopped and gasped for breath. *No!* she thought. *No!*

Her father came out of their hut and saw her. He rushed towards her and held her to his chest.

"I'm sorry, Zambia!" he cried. "Zambia, child, I'm so sorry! But your mother..."

Zambia broke away from him and staggered over to the arena. Empty. She stumbled into the tall grass screaming, "Zitza! Zitza!" frantically scanning the field for black-and-white stripes. "Zitza!"

Zambia shot off at a run, still screaming, until she fell onto soft grass. She pressed her face into the ground and tore at the plants with feverish hands. *When I look up she'll be there, grazing in our special place,* she thought.

Slowly she lifted her head. Nothing. She was alone. Her head dropped back onto the ground, her body shaking with sobs. *No, no, no! Not gone! Not my Zitza!*

Zambia stayed there until it got dark. Finally she dragged herself back to the hut. She had to pass Zitza's hide.

She remembered how she used to count her stripes and wonder, "Zitza, are you black with white stripes or white with black stripes?"

Zambia turned away. She couldn't bear it! How could they kill her? Her *best* friend? They had eaten her like *jackals!*

Suddenly furious, she charged into her hut. But when she entered, Zambia stopped abruptly, for sitting up, her eyes bright and her body nourished, was her mother.

Zambia rushed into her arms and held her close.

"Your Zitza saved me," said her mother. "She saved us all."

Zambia could see tears in her eyes and in her father's. She could feel them running down her own cheeks as well.

Because of Zitza, her mother wouldn't starve. In a way, Zitza would still be with Zambia, for her spirit would live on in her mother. Zambia hugged her mother again, bringing her father in too. Suddenly they heard a noise on the thatched roof.

Plip.

Then another.

Plop.

And more and more. Zambia rushed outside to see what was going on—and got a face full of water! Wiping her eyes, she gazed up at the sky, letting the drops fall onto her hot, dusty skin. Zambia opened her dry lips to let the water slide down her parched throat, sending out a prayer of thanks to whatever god had finally had mercy on them. *Thank you, thank you, THANK you!*

Comet Is Missing

by Annakai Hayakawa Geshlider, age 12

MY CAT, COMET, has always lived the wild life, ever since we adopted him as a kitten. We let him roam free outside, he won't allow a collar, he catches birds and mice to eat, he uses no litter box.

I had the worst of bad feelings on Sunday afternoon when I realized that Comet was nowhere to be found. The thought crossed my mind that maybe we shouldn't have been so easy-going about letting him out onto the city streets, especially at night. Both the closets and the dryer were empty, and there was no ball of fur on the bed or on top of the clay-firing kiln in our basement. I felt a deep pit in my stomach and I thought about where he might be out there. He was a small tabby cat and the world was unimaginably huge in comparison.

That night I lay in bed, sobbing and unsure what to do. Comet could be anywhere, in a car down the road, stuck in a garden, or maybe—I forced myself not to think about it—maybe even dead.

The next morning I awoke and rubbed away dry tears. I felt

Annakai was living in San Francisco, California, when her story appeared in the July/August 2008 issue of Stone Soup.

THE STONE SOUP BOOK

horrible about all the times that I clapped loudly to scare Comet off the computer desk, or the times when he nipped me because of the ways I'd patted him or brushed him. He was surely a very sensitive cat, but I felt guilty about his disappearance.

I spent the early part of the morning posting flyers around my neighborhood that my dad had designed the night before.

Comet Is Missing!
If you've seen this rascal,
please let us know.
He could be sleeping in your yard, eating your food,
but he's
Wanted by the Authorities

The poster offered a reward and listed a phone number. Centered on the page was Comet, just his head showing when the picture was taken of him in a brown paper bag. The color reproduction of the photo looked so real; I yearned to reach out and touch his soft, short fur. In the picture he looked so cute with his large green eyes and little pink nose. His expression was so innocent-seeming, which made me think of the times that I got up early in the morning, and Comet would swat my feet and bite my ankles out of eagerness for his food. Innocent. Yeah right, I thought, and almost smiled.

As the morning grew older, I put Comet's face all over the neighborhood, on telephone poles, light posts, and in the window of the local pet store. Wherever I looked, I saw my lost cat's face. I will not give up hope of finding him, I told myself.

I was in higher hopes when I answered the phone that afternoon and learned that someone might have found Comet. A friend of a friend had found a cat whom he was keeping at his house. I hung up the phone and prayed that it would be him.

The San Francisco weather was breezy yet warm when I walked across the street to the light green apartment building where this person lived. I entered the building and scaled a flight of red-carpeted stairs, taking them two at a time. The suspense was too much to bear.

I was led into a bright kitchen, where food and water bowls were laid carefully on the linoleum with a litter box nearby. We went into the living room where there were couches and a view of the street. Then my eyes landed on a cat lying atop a bookshelf in the corner.

For a split second my heart sank and I lost hope. "That's not him," I said confidently, eyeing the feline who had just begun to wake up after a nap in a sun patch. But as the cat got up, the moment of realization made me ecstatic. It was Comet! He hopped down for a pat on the back, and I fed him a chicken treat that I'd brought from the cupboard at home. I couldn't stop stroking him with immense pleasure; it was all too good. It turned out that Comet had somehow gotten onto the roof of the apartment, and had gotten stuck in the light well. "My upstairs neighbor heard him meowing all night, so I found him and brought him in," said the man who had rescued Comet.

After gratefully thanking him, I gently picked Comet up and carried him down the stairs and back across the street. I felt the hard asphalt on my feet as I kept Comet in the firm cradle of my arms. Now that I had been reunited with him, I felt as if I could never let him go, but I decided to put him down once we reached the opposite sidewalk because of his restlessness.

When he reached the concrete, Comet seemed unsure for a moment and stood still, and I was unsure as to whether he wanted to go home, or if he had no care for it anymore. I began to jog to encourage him forward, and right away he broke into a full-out cheetah run. When we reached our house, Comet skidded on the concrete and came to an abrupt stop, only to continue running, taking the front stairs of my house by twos. He was so happy to be home; he beat me to the front door by a couple of yards. He always does.

Rumor

by Hugh Cole, age 12

FRIGID WIND WHIPS through my long brown hair and bites me with cold teeth. It carries the strong smell of the sea in it, which stings my nose. Gray, salty water is churned into waves by the gale and sprinkles my chilly bare feet that are sinking into the wet sand. A seagull struggles to fly to its nest. I watch the large bird as it finally defeats the wind and lands in a small hollow high on a weathered rock.

I sniff, disappointed by the wind, then turn around and walk up the beach, avoiding flurries of gritty sand. Huge rocks like the one the seagull is perching on stud the beach and reach into the sky like the rough fingers of an old man.

I come to the gravel road leading away from the beach and the sea and awkwardly hobble across it, not wanting to press my feet too hard against the sharp little rocks. I walk across a lawn of grass that is long and plush like a carpet.

As I enter my small house, I welcome the warmth and savor the familiar smell.

Hugh was living in Moscow, Idaho, when his story appeared in the January/February 2010 issue of Stone Soup.

"Is that you, Nicole?" my mom calls from the kitchen.

"Yes." I enter the steamy room and sit at the table. My mom is at the stove, grilling the sea bass my brother, Brent, caught that morning for dinner.

"Why back so soon?" She starts humming a pretty tune as she adds spices from glass shakers.

"The wind is too cold," I groan miserably.

"I thought it might be," Mom says knowingly, looking at me. I see that she is wearing her peach-colored apron. It has the handprints of Brent, Zoë, and me on it in red paint. Mine are smaller than my two older siblings'.

"It seems it always is," I say, fiddling with the zipper of my jacket.

"Well, that's Maine's beaches for you," she sighs. I nod in agreement. Maine's beaches are always cold and windy.

I get up from the table and walk down the narrow hallway that leads to my room. School pictures of us three kids hang on the walls alongside my dad's fishing boat, a large, proud vessel. Mom and Dad are standing next to each other in the bow of the boat, squinting in sunlight yet smiling.

I enter my room, which is small like the rest of the house. Sand dollars of various sizes and hues are tacked to the walls, and the bedside table, desk, and dresser are all covered in dark, glossy seashells which I have collected along the beach and in tide pools. Several of my watercolor paintings add to the decoration, resting on the sea-green walls. They are mostly of the sea, but there are a few lighthouses as well.

My bed is messy and unmade, as it usually is. I let myself fall onto it. I punch my pillow a couple times and lay my head down sideways. In this position I can see my painting of the large sky-blue lighthouse. It is taller and wider than most lighthouses, and unlike the rest of my paintings, it actually exists. I discovered it one day while exploring along the beach. It is old and rickety, abandoned, with wide sheets of wiry ivy growing on it. I think the ivy looks like it's strangling the lighthouse, so I left that part out when I painted it a few weeks ago.

That night, after dinner, and after I have brushed my teeth with thick toothpaste, my sister, Zoë, and I sit in the living room and look out the big window. We stare at the choppy waters, illuminated by the pale moon that sits in a throne of twinkling stars. The light of the moon dances on the water, glittering brightly.

"The sea is so beautiful," Zoë murmurs, tucking a loose strand of her hair behind her ear. I pull a blanket draped over the back of an armchair and wrap it snuggly around myself.

"I know," I agree, "especially in the night."

THE NEXT DAY the wind has stopped. I am relieved and return to the beach, after Mom tells me to stay away from the water and be safe. Despite the wind's absence, it is still cold. The sun shyly peeks through thin, stretched clouds, providing no warmth.

Instead of heading back home, I start the short journey to the blue lighthouse. It is hidden in a small bay that has huge boulders blocking the entrance from the sea. Large trees grow around it, hiding it like a leafy wall.

There is no door to the lighthouse, just rusty hinges connected to an empty frame. The sky-blue paint is faded and peeling, revealing cracked wood and rusty nails. The inside of the lighthouse is hollow and dim. I am sure there used to be doors and floors, but now it is just one large room that leads up to a glass roof, for the large light is gone too. A few bird nests are built on the wall, but I don't hear anything from them.

A squeak brings my attention to the floor of the lighthouse, which is dirt and weeds now. A small ferret is looking at me cautiously. I can see its small legs are tensed, ready to run. I freeze, not wanting to scare it or make it angry. I am afraid it might be rabid.

The ferret takes one step nearer to me. It seems to relax.

It is brown and skinny with a long tail tipped with black. It has dark eyes ringed with white fur, as are its ears. I'm not sure if it is a boy or a girl, but I'll pretend it's a boy.

"What's your name?" I ask thoughtfully. My voice echoes in the lighthouse. "Is it… Rumor?" I realize using the word as a name is odd, but I like the sound of it. I kneel down to him, all thoughts of him being dangerous gone. My movement seems to frighten Rumor, and he hisses and scampers off, running through my legs and out into the cold day. I turn and watch him.

Suddenly, a bird with dark, russet-colored feathers and a sharp beak thuds into the ground with outstretched talons next to Rumor, sending a plume of sand into the air. I yelp in surprise, as well as fear for the ferret. The bird appears to be some kind of hawk. I see the bird struggle to grab Rumor with its wicked talons. I run out onto the beach, waving my arms and yelling. The hawk's attention is momentarily on me. Rumor must sense this, for he scurries out of the hawk's grip and runs into the woods that fringe the beach. The bird pursues, and I grab a few small pebbles and dash into the woods. I immediately lose sight of the hawk, and I search desperately for Rumor. I hear a commotion a few feet away and see the hawk crying angrily into a hollow log. I throw one pebble at it but miss. Luckily, the stone startles the bird, and it backs off. I throw the other pebbles. They all miss, but they drive the hawk off. It flaps off into the sky, cawing in frustration.

I find I am exhausted and fall to my knees into a patch of ferns. Rumor comes out from the hollow log and looks cautiously for the hawk. He cocks his head then sees me. I think he'll run from me, being the timid thing he is. But instead he slowly comes towards me. I reach out my finger and pet his neck, delighted at how soft his fur is. The ferret makes a sound that is much like the purring of a cat, and if ferrets smile, I'm sure that is what Rumor is doing. I pet him with my entire hand now, smoothing down the unsettled fur. He eventually runs away, leaving me with a smile on my face. I stand up and walk back out to the beach, then begin the journey home.

I tell no one in my family about Rumor or the hawk, just

for the sake of having a secret. But I tell paper and paint about Rumor, using a thin brush as my tongue. The painting shows a small ferret with a black-tipped tail, running from a fierce hawk. I hang it on the wall once it has dried.

I return to the spot in the woods, the place with the disturbed patch of ferns and the hollow log, in a few days, just to see if Rumor is still there. But he is not. I am slightly upset but not terribly. It is what I expected. I sit outside the lighthouse, staring at the bay. It is not windy, so the gray water is relatively calm. I then jump to my feet, excited, for I notice it is warm. The sun is out, and it is warm! I run out onto the beach, leaving the sky-blue lighthouse behind. I laugh with joy and spread my arms out and spin in circles, leaving a spiral in the sand. And as I turn to go home, to tell Mom it is warm, I am not sure, but I think I see a black-tipped tail dart through bushes out of the corner of my eye.

Memories of Moon

by Abbie Brubaker, age 13

WHEN THE WIND blows on a funeral, it cries with the heartbroken. It mourns with the tearful. It drops bright leaf handkerchiefs from its shaking fingers. When the wind watches as a coffin is lowered into the ground, it bows its gray head in sorrow. And even as the last regretful people get into their cars to leave, the wind stays a moment longer, fingering the fresh grave, before whipping away to think of what it has witnessed.

But when the wind blew on Moon's funeral, it didn't cry. It didn't mourn. It didn't even need a handkerchief. The coffin it should have watched was too small for its tastes, the mourners too few for it to even deem this a proper funeral. After all, it was spring, and the wind was no more than a lazy-boy breeze, blowing loose things around like a bored child kicking at tin cans. The wind didn't care about Moon. But I did.

MOON HAD HER START as a small white kitten in a pathetic little "Free to Good Home" basket at a yard sale. Mom and

Abbie was living in Lancaster, Pennsylvania, when her story appeared in the May/June 2008 issue of Stone Soup.

Daly were digging through piles of stained clothing and broken toys as I wandered around, bored out of my wits. Yard sales were ridiculous to me, like saying, "Here, take this stuff. It's so gross I don't want it anymore," or "We were too fussy to sell our stuff on eBay, so we'll sell it here at the same outrageous price." I had just skirted a large haystack of skis and bent ski poles when I saw the basket. It was across the street, at the very foot of the driveway, too obvious that these kittens were unexpected and unwanted.

I was a cat lover born and bred, growing up in a house where it was impossible to wear anything black in public or to escape the dreaded litter-box routine. I was totally ready to bring another member into the family, as one of our three cats, Smoky, had died of old age just a few months before. So when I saw that basket, there wasn't anything to stop me. I practically plowed over Mason, the neighbor's seven-year-old, as he stood in front of the basket. He looked up at me with big sweet eyes and asked, "Do you want one, Jackie? Mommy says that they've all got to go today." How could I resist? Carefully, I inspected each of the darling little creatures. They were all white but one, which was gray. I was drawn immediately to the gray one. *He likes to stand out from the crowd*, I thought in amusement. However, I could see that he was skittish and shy of people, backing away from my hand as far as he could. Mom would never let me make a project out of accustoming him to people, so I turned to the next. That was Moon. She was as friendly as her brother was nervous, and I was able to pick her up and rub my fingers through her silky kitten fur. She was the one for me.

"NO, JACKIE. Absolutely not." That was Mom's first reaction to Moon.

I begged, "But Mom, Smoky's been gone for *months*, and I need another cat in the house to complete our trio."

"We don't need any more vet bills than we already have. Vaccinations cost money, and we're still paying off Smoky's heart medication." She looked down at Daly and held up a hideous pink T-shirt with orange fringe that I strongly suspected had been white when the shirt was new-bought. "How's this, Daly?" Mom asked, changing the subject.

Daly hopped up and down, babbling as only a four-year-old can: "Mommy, Mommy, my shirt! My pink shirt!" Mom looked satisfied and slung the shirt over a growing pile on her left arm.

"So can we, Mom?" I asked, thinking she might be in a better mood now. "Can we?"

"No."

My attempts to persuade her failed miserably for several minutes, until my stroke of genius saved the day. I was dragging my feet as Mom flipped through racks of women's clothes. Daly, likewise, was whining and sighing with boredom. Then it hit me. Slyly, I asked, "Hey, Daly, do you want to see a kitty?"

She faced me, pouting. "We've got kitties already. I want to see toys!"

"But we don't have kitties like *this*." I took her hand, careful not to pull too hard, and added, "They're a lot smaller than Oreo and Tiger. Come on, let me show you!" She finally stopped digging in her heels and, reluctantly, followed me across the street.

Her hesitance evaporated when she spotted the kittens in the basket. With a squeal that made Mason cover his ears, she pounced on the gray kitten and was about to scoop him up when I quickly tugged her hand away.

"No, that one is scared, Daly. Look at this one." I placed her small fingers on Moon's head, and the kitten, playing her part perfectly, began to purr and rub against Daly's hand. My sister was enchanted.

"Jackie, let's get this one," she cried, and I didn't stop her when she picked up this kitten. I trusted Daly with holding cats; like me, she had grown up surrounded by them— Dragon, Floss, Smoky, and our remaining cats, Oreo and Tiger. Triumphantly, I led Daly and her precious bundle back across the street, where I faced Mom with a grin.

"And thus, our new kitten joins the family." I gestured to my sister. Daly proudly held up the small white kitten. Mom really did try to rally her forces and resist, but her genes and mine were too closely linked. She was as much a cat lover as her daughters.

"All right. We'll keep it. Boy or girl, and what's its name?"

"Girl." I closed my eyes for a moment to think of a good name and the image of the kitten's face, round and white as a full moon, slid behind my eyelids. I looked at Mom with an even larger smile. "Her name is Moon."

I REMEMBER the night we discovered Moon's worst fear. She was about three months old, a family cat, who got along well with Oreo and Tiger. She was also my favorite. That terrifying night, I was curled on my bed with a mystery novel, a bowl of chocolate pudding, and a cat. Outside my window, the storm was just getting underway, with a gale blowing and rain pounding the glass. Moon purred comfortably in my ear, as if she knew that the storm wouldn't be able to hurt her while she was in here with me. Of course, that was when the first thunderclap came. *KA-BOOM!*

It was the loudest I had ever heard, making me jump and almost spill my snack. But Moon didn't just jump; she *flew.* I think she must have hit the ceiling, then she hot-footed it out of there like a flash. Another clap of thunder, softer this time, drew a high-pitched yowl from the bathroom. I put down my book, carefully placed my bowl on the bedside table, and went looking for Moon. See, I knew that some cats had irrational fears—Tiger wouldn't touch any body of water larger than his dish, my grandma's cat, Mint, absolutely cowered before dogs—so this wasn't too surprising for me. "Moon?" I called, flipping on the bathroom light. She was crouched behind the toilet, all her fur standing on end, her green eyes flashing with terror. I made a slow movement forward, murmuring, "It's all right, Moon. It's OK," over and over. Moon gave a shiver, though she stayed in place. I could see that her fur was beginning to lie flat as I came closer; she seemed ready to come to me when, from the bathroom window, I saw a huge flare of lightning. Oh dear, I thought, knowing what would come next. In the split second between the lightning and the thunder, I slammed the bathroom door to keep Moon from escaping. And *then* the power went out.

When the thunder hit, it was loud enough to make me wince, no comparison to what it did to Moon. She sounded ready to break down the door, running around like a maniac, hissing and spitting. I could see her glowing green eyes in the dark, and for the first time, I was afraid of a cat. "Moon," I said shakily, trying to reassure her. There was nothing of the old Moon left to reassure. I jumped up on the toilet and decided that I would just have to wait it out.

The storm lasted for a good half hour, the power staying off until around 11:00 P.M.; by the time the last thunder rumbled away, Moon was exhausted and I was shaking. As the lights flickered back on and I finally got down from my perch, she came up to me, giving a tired little meow. I gathered her into my arms and hugged her tight. That first crazy storm was the worst ever during the time Moon was with us. After that, we learned to keep her in a small space with a comforting person, usually me, when the thunder came. Even when I had learned her fear, I loved her more than ever.

I ALSO REMEMBER the time she almost drowned. Moon didn't mind water, and in the summer we'd sometimes go wading in the slow creek that was back behind our house. She would come along, and I'd lower her gently into the water. By the time a few first trial runs had taken place, she had figured out a sort of cat's doggy-paddle and could out-swim Daly. It was the summer I turned fourteen, when Moon was about two years old. We went down to the creek, me in my tankini, Daly in her flowery little one-piece and water wings, and Mom in her capri pants. Mom didn't do much wading, even in steamy August.

"Jackie, look at me!" cried Daly, splashing furiously up and down in the sluggish water. From the bank, dabbling my feet in the water with Moon sitting beside me, I nodded at her.

"I see you. You're doing good." Apparently excited by Daly's efforts, Moon jumped right in, leaving me to laugh and cheer. Mom was on the other bank, and together we acted as a sort of lifeguard, calling out occasionally, "Daly, let go of Moon, you'll pull her down," or "Daly, kick a little harder and you'll go faster!"

Farther downstream was a section of rocks and currents that Mom had forbidden us to go near, though it wasn't strong enough to pull me down anymore. It was certainly strong enough, however, to pull down a small, white cat. On that hot day, we were too busy trying to coach Daly in her swimming techniques to notice when Moon set off to explore. I yelled, "Come on, use your arms!" Daly looked up and glared at me, spitting water. "I'm trying, Jackie." She turned in a slow circle, allowing herself to be carried by the slow waters towards the rocks.

"Daly, come away from there," called my mom anxiously. Daly didn't respond, instead going closer to the stones and twirling waters. "Daly! Now!" Mom was standing up, yelling, her fists clenching with worry.

"But Moon's over here!"

"What?" The voice was mine. Daly continued floating downstream, and Mom looked over at me, but I was already in the water. With strong strokes I passed Daly, pausing to shove her away from the danger zone, then I dove under. Swimming as fast as I could in the general direction of the place where two rocks formed a deep cleft, I was panicking with the thought that Moon had been out of my sight for at least five minutes. It was impossible to see anything in the murky creek; I felt around furiously with my hands, wondering, How long has Moon been under? Is she even still alive? Oh let her be safe, please... My hands were scratched and scraped by the rocks by the time I touched fur. Grabbing the furry object with both hands, I pulled it the few inches to the surface. Moon's lifeless body was plastered wet and small in the dappled light. I screamed, "MOM!" She came running through the water, not even bothering to roll up her pants. Taking one look, she grabbed Moon out of my battered hands and jumped out of the water.

Mom was in the car heading to the vet in minutes, Daly and I barely managing to get in our seats before she drove away. Like I said, Mom is just as much a cat lover as I am. Doctor Peter Handsen, our trusty vet for all our cats, made dripping-wet Daly and me sit in the waiting room while he and Mom closed the door behind them. My little sister looked up at me with frightened eyes. "Is Moon dead?"

"*No!*" I saw instantly from the hurt in her face that my momentary anger had scared her. As big as she was, I picked her up and hugged her. "She's not dead. Doctor Handsen will make sure she's OK."

It was a long time in that waiting room. I watched the clock, counting the seconds, the minutes... Daly just stared at her bare feet. We were hungry and scared by the time the door opened again and Mom came out. Her eyes were so solemn and grim that for one heart-stopping moment I thought I had been too late in rescuing Moon. Then Mom smiled gently. "She's going to make it." I squeaked with joy and hugged Mom so hard she gasped. Daly wrapped herself around Mom after I was done, and Mom picked her up, adding, "Doctor Handsen is keeping her overnight to make sure she hasn't caught anything, but he says she's a tough kitty. She'll make it." I admit it, I cried, right there in the waiting room, with a wet-dog smell in the air and the receptionist behind the desk snapping her gum. Mom gave me another hug and dried my tears on her shirt.

"Let's go home."

When Moon was returned the next day, she seemed thinner than before. We had to give her pills that she absolutely loathed, we had to make sure she stayed out of any drafts, and we had to keep her quiet for a week. Moon didn't want to be quiet. She unrolled toilet paper from the downstairs bathroom; she knocked over Mom's favorite vase, which landed luckily on the carpet; she wanted to play every moment of that whole week she was supposed to be "kept quiet." Moon was never a cat to be too obliging.

NOW I REMEMBER the past few weeks, all silent in our house, started by that one loud event which took Moon away from us. I was enjoying spring break, a few days of rest before launching into the last desperate leg of the school year. The morning it happened was blissful with peace, until the first scenes of the disaster began to play out. The phone had been ringing, Mom trying to answer it, coming in from the patio through the screen door with a scrub brush in one hand and a bucket of soapy water for scouring the tiles dangling from the other. Moon was lying on the arm of Dad's favorite chair, her eyes only half closed. When I think of it, I realize that she was probably not asleep at all, just waiting for Mom to open the door. That chair was directly across from the screen door.

Mom, rushing, yelling, "It's for me—don't get it!" banged through the door, leaving it half open. I was sitting on the couch, reading another mystery novel, when Moon bolted. She made it through the doorway, onto and off of the patio, and almost into the road before I threw down my book and followed her at a dead run.

"MOON!" She was an indoor cat, strictly indoor, never to be let out; I threw the door open wider as I pushed out into the spring air. Wet grass slipped under my feet and I fell, biting my tongue, still calling after my cat. "Moon, come back!"

I didn't see the car, but I heard it. A squeal of brakes, a horrible crunch, and a yowl that I had never heard before. Gasping, half-crazed with fear, I managed to skid into the road. "MOON!" I yelled again, my voice torn by shock this time as I saw the scene. A lump of white fur, stained red, in the road, overshadowed by a huge, boxy car. The driver was leaning out his window, calling, "I didn't see it! Sorry!" Before I could say anything to him, he reversed, then drove around the tiny, lifeless body in the middle of the road, and disappeared over the hill.

Just as when Moon had almost drowned, I screamed for my mother. There was a slam, a clatter, then she emerged from the house, looking totally freaked out. I played back my own voice in my mind and realized I sounded as if I was the one who was hurt.

"Jackie, what's wrong?" As she spoke the words, she saw Moon.

"Oh my," she gasped, then stopped still. Wordless. Breathless. Then she was in motion again, silent motion that brought her to Moon, then back to me with Moon wrapped in her jacket. She spoke in a voice that scared me, it was so cold. "Call Doctor Handsen, Jackie. Right now."

I don't remember calling the vet. I don't remember actually getting into the car with Mom in the driver's seat and Moon in my lap. I remember the car ride, though. We sped through scanty afternoon traffic, cold silence between me and my mother. It wasn't that we were mad at each other, it was just that we were both so afraid for Moon… I felt like if I said anything, she'd slip away. As it was, she was barely breathing, her eyes closed, no hint of the energy she usually had. Blood was seeping through the towel Mom had grabbed on our way out, and I tried to ignore it. I wasn't trembling exactly, only giving an occasional shudder, and I never took my eyes off Moon. We were at the vet's office in hardly a moment, yet it seemed hours to me. Just as had happened before, Mom and Doctor Handsen were about to close the door to the examination room behind them, and leave me to wonder and wait in agony, but I stopped them.

"Let me come." It wasn't a question, and for a moment I thought Mom would be angry at me for saying it. Then she nodded, and Doctor Handsen nodded, and we all entered the steel-shiny room. I sat down in a chair against the far wall and watched.

I thought I would die myself when I saw the blood. Moon's blood, staining the metal table. Doctor Handsen shook his head as he peeled back Moon's eyelids and checked her breathing. He did more things, but I was too shaken up to understand what they were. It was cold in the examination room, deathly cold, a feeling I didn't want around me. Mom and Doctor Handsen talked in hard voices that were too quiet for me to hear the words; both adults' voices sounded to me like metallic bumblebees, droning with a dulled edge of despair. In a dreamlike state, I wondered if Daly had any idea of what happened. Her school didn't have spring break, so she would be in a classroom somewhere with the orderly life of elementary-school days around her, pencils and little kids who teased each other in a one-big-family way. Did the man who hit Moon have children in Daly's school? Would he drive his big boxy car to pick them up? And would Daly somehow understand that he had killed our cat? *Almost* killed, I reminded myself sternly. Shuddering, shivering, I looked over at the two adults next to the examining table, and did a double-take. *No... It couldn't be true.* Mom was crying. That shook me right down to my toes; Mom didn't cry. She wasn't that kind of person—she was a Wonder Woman, strong as iron, ready for anything.

"Mom?" My voice was soft and ragged, a tiny piece of broken glass among all those shiny metal surfaces. "What's wrong?"

"Her injuries are too severe, Jackie," said Doctor Handsen gravely. "I'm afraid Moon is dead."

It was as if, by saying those words, "Moon is dead," he unleashed every horrible feeling I've ever had in my life. It wasn't just sorrow, it was anger like when our first cat had to be put down, it was rebellion like the first time Mom sent me to my room, it was shock like when Moon had almost drowned—all mixed up into something equivalent to a witch's brew of emotion. The angry part of me screamed, *Doctor Handsen should have been able to save her!*, while the rebellion muttered, *Moon can't be dead, she can't be dead,* even as shock blurred everything in my sight. Or maybe that was tears, when I stumbled to the examination table and saw for myself the motionless body, stained red with blood and black with dirt from the road. *Moon is dead,* I realized dazedly. That put a stop to all the other emotions raging inside me. *Moon is dead.*

AND HERE I AM now, at a funeral with only three other mourners: Mom, Dad, and Daly. With only the heartless, fleeting wind for a pastor, and only memories left. Only memories... memories of Moon.

Badger Will Be Badger

by Bailey Bergmann, age 12

NOBODY KNEW why we kept him. To tell the truth, I didn't exactly know, either. We named him Badger for the brown-gold stripe that ran down his muzzle, and later on, we would say that it fit his personality, too. He wasn't exactly an aggressive dog. He was, however, a jumpy, biting, rebellious dog. But he was beautiful and cute, and we loved him. Mom once commented, "It's a good thing he's so adorable…" She'd always trail off, whether to add emphasis or to search for words, I don't know.

Badger was a male version of Miss Congeniality and probably the most well-loved mutt among the people at the puppy training class, too, for Badger was Prince Charming in fur. He was always happy around new people, always wagging his tail, always squirming for attention.

That personality was his downfall. Sure, he was cute. My younger sister Sierra was always shrieking, "Isn't he *adorable?!!*"

The youngest, Clarabelle, would always chime in, "I know; he's the cutest."

Bailey was living in Shawano, Wisconsin, when her story appeared in the March/April 2008 issue of Stone Soup.

I, however, demanded discipline and respect. They demanded cuteness. He was good at that. Good, I mean, at looking cute with pillows in mouth, Kleenexes shredded all around him, and towels slobbered upon.

At first, we thought it was just puppy energy. But as he grew into a big, strong, naughty golden retriever, we quickly changed our thinking. Wherever Badger roamed, trouble was to follow. Anyone who had to live with Badger knew that...

I CLAMPED the hand brake back, and wiped a hand across my brow. It was late March, but the snow was all melted away, the temperature in the high eighties, and the river unfrozen. As I rested on my bike, I gazed at the crystal-blue water through the thick sumacs. Thin layers of ice still covered some of the Wolf River, but most of it was thawed. Ducks, geese, and sea gulls rested on the remaining ice, making a loud racket that was a mixture of honks, croaks, and shrieks sounding like women screaming.

"Amazing," I breathed. I had lived in Wisconsin for several years, but I was always dazzled by the river in springtime. I got a good view, too. My house was situated about fifty feet from Stumpy Bay's bank, and the bank was surrounded by sumac trees and long, itchy grass. Stumpy Bay was where we got our water supply (filtered, of course), but it was off-limits for swimming. Stumpy Bay was named for the deadheads, algae, quicksand, muskies, and snapping turtles that lurked in the murky water. In the spring, it was clear and blue, like the rest of the river, but in the summer, it was covered in a film of green algae, which looked disgusting. It also smelled horrible, especially on muggy days.

"Come on, Lu!" Sierra was calling, speeding down the gravel driveway with Badger at her wheels. "Beat you to the road!"

"Just try!" I shouted back, digging my feet into the pedals. I easily caught up with Sierra, and we both nearly collided with Clarabelle and Badger, who were coming back. Sierra and I turned around carefully and then raced back, laughing light-heartedly. Badger had dropped back to my spokes, for he was becoming winded from the exercise. Of cou Badger did love me rse, everywhere Badger went, mischief was involved. That's why my skirt was muddied by Badger's dirty lips and my leg had a scratch from some stray teeth.

"Git, dog!" I yelled, thoroughly sick of having to discipline this unintelligent mutt. Badger looked at me daringly with his hazel-brown eyes. He moved closer again, and I was tempted to run straight into him and teach him a lesson, but refrained. A bite on my leg was the reward for my mercy.

"*Badger!*" I braked so suddenly that I nearly flipped off. I threw my bike down and lunged toward the puppy, whose tail was wagging in merriment. "No, don't give me that 'I don't care' look!" I hissed. Badger danced on his legs, eyes twinkling. My anger boiled even more at his nonchalant attitude. "Do you want to go up? Do you want a spanking? Do I have to drag you to your kennel?"

Badger wasn't the least bit subdued, and immediately turned around and ran off to Sierra and Clarabelle, who were slurping down Gatorade. Tears stung my eyes as I picked up my bike and slung my helmet onto the handle.

Why care? I thought. He doesn't. I pour my life into him, trying to make him happy, and all he does is attack me. Why? Why does he prefer Sierra over me, when I am the one who regulates what he does and does not do? I was jealous, hot, and upset. I loved Badger; where was the love I deserved? I had read story after story about how dogs were the most loyal friends a girl could have, but where did Badger fit into this category? I had had so many high hopes of him becoming a therapy dog, or an agility competitor, but he couldn't even sit for two seconds.

I walked my bike back up the driveway, Sierra and Clarabelle both asking what was wrong. I ignored them—and Badger—and parked my bike in the garage sullenly.

If he hates me, I decided, then I will hate him too. I glanced at Badger one more time, then turned and left him, slipping into the house and slamming the door shut.

I stomped up to my room and threw myself onto my bed, glaring at the design on my pillowcase. I looked up above my bed where a framed photograph of Badger and me hung. Daddy had snapped it when Badger first came home; when he was arm-sized, cuddly soft, and oh-so-sweet. I was smiling—my cheek buried into the top of his fuzzy, honey-colored head, my left arm wrapped around his chubby chest, the other supporting his bottom. His eyes were squinted, nothing like the expressive eyes Badger now had. His tongue wasn't hanging out sideways or cracked in a Badger-grin. He was perfect. Too perfect. I angrily reached up and yanked it down, intending to toss it in my drawer to forget forever. As it was clenched in my hands, however, I couldn't keep my gaze off that dog. He was the picture of innocence, of calmness, of a well-behaved dog, but that's not what captivated me. I couldn't quite grasp it at first, but then it hit me. This wasn't my baby—it wasn't Badger. Badger was Badger—no human intervention could change that. What would this house be like without Badger? What would it be like with a perfect doll dog?

I struggled with the answer, trying to push away the truth. It would be terrible, I finally admitted. There would be no Badger to knock you down with his oversized sticks; no Badger to see that your arm was never not scratched; no Badger to bark nonstop whenever he wanted out of his kennel. Without Badger, who would eat the rest of the cat's breakfast? Who would alter your wardrobe to rags? Who would you baby talk to whenever you entered the house?

My anger and unforgiveness melted like ice on the river. Badger was just like me—he needed to be molded, directed and disciplined, and most importantly, he needed to be loved. A wave of guilt passed over me, and I leaned my head against the picture frame, thinking hard. Even if Badger never did lie still for three seconds, he was still Badger. Badger would remain Badger. But he was a puppy, a baby. He was not yet brilliant, nor was he fully trained. His main goal in life was to please himself, but perhaps later on he would realize that the hands that fed him and petted him, and the hearts that loved him were the ones to be gratified. Badger had a big heart. It was easy for me to see that. The hyper-dog would transition into one of unconditional loyalty. Badger *did* love me. He was just expressing it in his own way.

With a new resolve and joyfulness, I skipped downstairs and opened the door. Badger, his teeth clamped on a red jump rope, looked my way. I laughed, my heart overflowing with love.

"Want to go on a walk, Beegie?" I called, using his pet name. We started down the driveway, Badger trotting in his horselike way in front, Sierra and Clarabelle following. I had a mind to go right, towards the main field and away from Stumpy Bay, since Badger did sometimes splash in water. But I found myself going left. I trusted Badger's sensibility, and even though he loved wading, swimming was not his style.

There was a break in the sumacs, and to the right, only a few trees grew here and there, so you could see the river clearly. A shallow area with only ankle-deep water washed over it, and rolled downward into the bay. I could see the bottom of it, but it ended in dark water; I couldn't see how deep it was over there, though I guessed over my head. Badger, being the water dog that he was, investigated the area promptly. We girls stayed on dry land, I scrutinizing his every move. I tensed as he came to the edge of the swamped-over mud patch and his forelegs sank deep into the water. Clarabelle, Sierra and I began jumping up and down, hollering in enticing voices for Badger to come back. We knew he wasn't in any immediate danger; he could swim (even if he didn't like to), and he was a smart dog, even with all his other faults. Sure enough, Badger wheeled around, looking pleased and refreshed, though he smelled terrible.

"Let's go back," I suggested. I didn't want to take any more chances with Mr. Badger.

"OK," Sierra agreed, picking up on my motherly instinct. "Come here, Beegie, Beegie, Beegie!"

We headed towards the driveway again, Badger galloping after us. Then, before I knew what was happening, Badger was streaking back towards the water.

My eyes widened in horror. "No, Badger!" I yelled, chasing after him, ignoring the sting of the grass on my bare legs and the mud that was splashing onto my flip-flops. Just like that, without a splash, my dog, my baby, disappeared into the water—simply vanished, rings of water rippling out from the place he had descended.

He was probably underwater for just a second, but time seemed to have frozen. I didn't know if anyone else said anything or moved, but I only heard my own voice screaming, "Badger!!" It was a high-pitched scream of horrific desperation. It couldn't have been my own.

Something drove me on in this time-frozen moment. I unconsciously propelled towards the water, my bare feet were now wet, my flip-flops caught in the muck. I stumbled over a tree root and unintentionally dove into Stumpy Bay, bobbing up with a gasp, thrashing around for dear life. It all happened in a few seconds, and Badger was soon up, too, his head held high above the water, struggling against the current. I could feel his legs pumping out the rhythm of my heart.

He was trying to come towards me, but the current was pulling him away.

"Good boy, over here." My voice was chopped from the chattering of my teeth. Badger's eyes rolled towards land.

"No, baby, look at me!" Tears were welling up, but they were blocking my view; I could not cry. "Badger!" I had to go under again. I emerged, my hair blocking my face. I tried to tread water with one hand as I cleared my face with the other, but it was difficult. I could not touch bottom; I didn't even know where bottom was. My sisters were screaming something, but I wasn't listening. My attention was focused on Badger, terrified, helpless. It cut to my heart, giving me a boost of power.

"I'm coming, Badger!" I gurgled as loudly as I could. He was an arm's length away from me. I stretched. My hand was instantly cut by one of his sharp claws. I barely felt the pain; it was numb anyway. My stiff fingers wrapped around his collar, and I pulled him close, being careful to avoid his claws. Now that I had him, I needed to get to land. The current was sweeping us towards the ice, and that meant we were heading for the river's middle, which meant fewer things to grab hold of, for only Stumpy Bay had things sticking up in the water. My eyes opened at this. Stumps! Of course! They didn't call Stumpy Bay *Stumpy Bay* for nothing. But where could I grab hold of one?

"Grab it, Lucy!" It was Sierra's faint voice shouting out this fateful command. Grab what? I looked around, not loosening my grip on Badger, and saw what Sierra was screaming about. It was a small stump, protruding out of the water. It looked thick enough, but the diameter was definitely not wide enough for both Badger and me. Still, it would keep us afloat. I grabbed, and my fingers touched the slimy, slippery wood. Gasping, I gripped it as my lifeline. I went into a sitting position, and helped Badger put his front legs on mine, so he could rest. We were both breathing heavily, thankful for the rest. I turned and called to Sierra, "Go get help!"

Sierra had already sent Clarabelle, but now she, too, turned and fled.

I tried to concentrate on holding the stump and lifting up Badger, but my legs were growing weak, as were my arms, and I was shivering beyond belief. Badger huddled up against me. I clung to his collar. If we were to float away again, we were going together. Minutes passed. No one appeared. Then my ears picked up the wail of sirens. Help was coming!

An ambulance, followed by a dive crew, pulled up onto our street. Mom was standing with Clarabelle and Sierra next to her. It was hard to see exactly what was going on, because Badger and I were a good way from shore.

"Help's coming, Badger," I whispered.

The inflatable boat cut into the cold, murky water, heading towards us. Badger began to whimper pitifully, but the only sound I made was the chattering of my teeth. Someone lifted me up, but I couldn't tell who. I didn't really look. I was soon out, wrapped in a thick blanket with Badger at my feet, bundled in one equally warm.

I fell into unconsciousness before I reached shore, and when I woke, I was in a prim, white hospital room. Mom and Daddy were looking at me anxiously, and I sat up, just as anxious.

"Lie down, sweetie," Mom crooned.

"Badger. Where's Badger?"

"Do you think a bit of water would hurt that dog?" Daddy teased.

A grin spread across my pale face. Of course not. After all, Badger *was* Badger.

Bullfighter

by William Gwaltney, age 12

IT'S A HOT, dry August evening on the Oklahoma panhandle. The sun is going down and the crickets have begun to sing. There's no breeze at all tonight, nothing to ease the blistering heat.

I am twenty-three years old. I finished four years of college before I realized that a banker's life was not for me. Right after graduation, I joined the PRCA, the Professional Rodeo Cowboys Association, and haven't looked back since. I've traveled across the country riding bulls... big, mean, strong bulls. But through it all, what I've really wanted is a different kind of rodeo job. Tonight I'm going to make my dreams a reality. I'll be one of two clowns at a local rodeo. Unlike circus clowns, rodeo clowns have a dangerous job. We're not just there to make the crowd laugh. During the bull riding, we become bullfighters, distracting the bulls to help keep the riders safe.

I slip into my costume. I pull on overalls that have had the legs cut out so they resemble a skirt. I need to be able to move freely

William was living in Englewood, Colorado, when his story appeared in the March/April 2008 issue of Stone Soup.

and turn fast. I pull on tights underneath to cover my legs. They are bright and colorful to attract the bulls' attention. I'll wear a cowboy hat but that goes on later. I begin to paint my face. It takes longer than anything else. As I am finishing up my makeup, I look into the mirror. I see my mother enter the room behind me.

Her lips tremble and her tense white fists are pressed together. Her face is pale and ghostlike. Her eyes plead with me. "Matthew," she says, "please listen to me. Don't do this, honey. I love you too much to see you put yourself in so much danger."

"But Mom," I tell her, "I don't really have a choice. This job chose me, remember?" The look in her eyes tells me that she remembers all too well. I walk across the room and wrap my arms around her.

I tell her that I am listening to her. That I really do understand her concerns. Then I tell her again that I really *must* do this. Not only for myself, but for Charlie too.

Just then, my father limps through the door to join us. Dad used to fight bulls. He'll understand. He smiles at me. Then he puts one hand on my shoulder and says, "All right, Matthew... ready to go?"

"Yeah, Pop," I tell him. I turn once more to my frightened mother and say, "All right, Mom, we're going now. Wish me luck." She pulls me close. She hugs me hard. She starts to cry. I tell her once again not to worry.

"Please be careful," she says. I'm not sure if she's crying for Charlie or for me. But then, I don't guess it really matters. I tell Dad that he can drive. We climb up into our rickety old Ford pickup. It is so badly rusted that its original color cannot be determined. My father bought it brand new in 1950. He says that it was black then, but you couldn't tell that by looking at it today.

It only takes ten minutes to drive to the local rodeo grounds. When we arrive, almost every seat is filled. The rodeo began over an hour ago, but bull riding is always the last event of the night. The bulls wait impatiently in small pens behind an iron gate.

THE STONE SOUP BOOK

There are Brahmas and Brahma crosses, Charolais, and scrappy Mexican fighting bulls. Their breed doesn't matter. All that matters is that they buck. There is only one given in bull riding. Those bulls will try to kick, trample and crush anything that's in their way, including me. I slide out of the truck and turn to my dad. "Now remember," he says "I'll be back to pick you up at ten o'clock. I'm going home so that I can be with your mother. If you need anything, call the house. Knock 'em dead, cowboy," he says to me, and then he is gone.

I spot my partner for tonight, another clown named Slim, and go to say hello. Along the way I pass cowboys who all greet me happily. Most don't know my name but they're glad to see me anyway. One look at my clothes tells them that I am a bullfighter. I will risk my life to grant them a few seconds of safety. They know that I will at least give them the chance to get up off the ground and run to the fence, avoiding danger.

In the chutes, they're getting the first bulls ready. A bull rope is slung around each bull's belly, and is snugged up right behind their front legs. One end of the rope is called the tail. It gets passed through a loop on the other end of the rope and then the rope is tightened. The cowboys then wrap the remainder of the tail around their hands to secure their grip. A sticky substance called rosin is applied to the tail to keep it from slipping. If you listen hard, you can hear the occasional clanging of cowbells as the bulls mill around in the chute. The bells are hung on the bull rope for weight. When a cowboy lets go of the rope, this weight will cause the rope to fall harmlessly to the ground, so that no one has to remove it from an angry bull. Later, when the bulls are turned loose and are bucking wildly, you can hear the cowbells easily. Of course, by then everyone is too distracted to even notice it.

The sun has gone down completely now as I walk out into the dusty arena. The first bull rider is preparing to climb aboard his bull. I secure my position, not too far away from the chute but not so close that I'll be in the way when it opens. I balance lightly on both feet, hands on my knees, ready to move fast in any direction. The lights glare above me. I am sweating but I can't tell if it's from the hot lights, the warm night, or the fear of knowing that in just a few seconds, a raging bull will be coming my way.

Suddenly, the gate swings open and out comes the first bull, bucking and angry. He would like nothing better than to kill the man on his back. The bull comes straight toward me, jumping and spinning. For a moment I am frozen in place. Everything seems to be moving in slow motion and all sounds are muffled. And then, all at once, I snap back to reality. I jump to the side just as the bull plunges by. I dodge and weave, staying close enough to the bull so that I can help the rider if he gets in trouble, but far enough away that the bull can't easily gore me. Just how long can eight seconds last? It seems as though I've been evading this bull forever.

Finally, the buzzer sounds. The good news is that this cowboy's time is up. Freeing his hand from the bullrope, the rider jumps off and that's my cue. As the bull turns to chase the cowboy, I jump between him and his intended prey. My brightly colored costume catches his eye and encourages him to come after me instead. I let the bull chase me, taunting him all the way, until I'm sure that the cowboy has gotten to the fence and out of harm's way. Then I change my position and run right past the bull's nose. He bellows in fury but can't change his own trajectory quickly enough. By the time he manages to change direction to come after me, I've put a good ten yards between us. Of course, for such a big animal with such a long stride, ten yards is nothing. I make it to the fence right before he does. As I jump up on the top rail, the bull slams into the fence. The fence shudders and so do I.

Suddenly I realize something. Slim is still in the arena. Caught up in what was going on, I never even noticed. Now that I am safe, however, I turn to see the bull charging my partner. He is far enough out toward the center of the arena that he doesn't have a chance of making it to the fence. I have to help him. I leap off the fence and sprint toward the bull for the second time. He wasn't very happy with me the first time, so I'm guessing he'll be even angrier now. The bull is closing in on Slim as I come up behind him. Grabbing the hat off of my head, I use it to smack him on the hindquarters. He slides to a stop and turns toward me, hatred in his eyes. Breathing heavily, he stands perfectly still and doesn't move. I dance forward, slap him again, and once more jump out of the way. He swings his heavy head, bellowing loudly, and begins to chase me. But now the fence is too far away for me to get to it as well. There's only one thing left to do.

The clown barrel is sitting in the middle of the arena. It's been called an island of safety by those in the rodeo business. I'm about to find out just how safe it really is. I run toward it and vault inside. I barely have time to curl into a ball and grab the handholds before the bull is upon me. Bam! Two new dents from the bull's mighty horns appear in the barrel right in front of my face. Then my barrel is spinning madly through the air. When it hits the ground again, it bounces several times before rolling across the arena. When it finally stops moving I'm dizzy and a little sick to my stomach.

As soon as my ears stop ringing, I shoot out of the barrel and make a mad dash to the fence. I grab the rails and climb for all I'm worth, not even daring to look behind me. I don't even notice when I reach the top of the fence. I attempt to keep climbing and fall over the top and onto the other side. I land on my back and look up at the stars. I hear the crowd. Half of the people are cheering, the other half are laughing. The laughing ones must think that this was all just a part of my act.

Two faces appear above me... Slim and the rodeo manager. "Thanks, Matthew," Slim tells me, "I reckon you saved my life."

"Any time," I say, panting. They get me up off the ground and help me back up onto the fence. Two men on horseback help to herd the bull out through the gate. The arena is clear once again. Slim and I climb down off the fence. The next bull to go is fighting so hard in the chute that his rider can't safely get on him.

Tension in the air is thick. It's time for a little comic relief.

I walk out to where the crowd can see me and to where I can interact with the announcer. At the top of my lungs I yell to the announcer, "What do you call a cow that don't give no milk?"

The announcer sits and ponders this for a moment. Then he says over the microphone, "I don't know. What do you call a cow that doesn't give any milk?"

I cup my hands around my mouth and yell, "A milk dud!" The crowd chuckles, but that's not enough for me. I want more of a response. I look over toward the chutes. The cowboy is still not on that bull. Now the bull is lying down and three cowboys are trying to get him back on his feet. I have a little extra time. I call to the announcer again. "Where is every cow's dream home?" I ask. He once again repeats the question back to me over the microphone so that the audience can hear. The answer, of course, is "Moo York." The crowd laughs out loud. I look toward the chutes again. It looks like there's time for one last joke. "What do you call a cow that's just had a calf?" I ask. Once again the announcer appears stumped. As I yell out, "Decaffeinated!" the audience roars with laughter. The tension is broken, and just in time too.

Now the bull is up and the rider is on him. I head back toward the chutes. I need to be ready when this bull comes out. After all, this bull, Bullet, is the reason I am here tonight. The gate swings open. Bullet doesn't move. He stands there, his eyes glaring, his sides heaving. I dance in front of him, hoping he'll charge out. He still doesn't move. Dancing in closer, I take off my hat and slap him across the muzzle, then dance back out of the way. When I was a kid watching Saturday morning cartoons, an enraged bull would narrow his eyes while steam poured from his nose. As I look at Bullet, I think I know where the animators got their ideas. Bullet suddenly explodes out of the chute, plunging straight toward me before he remembers the man on his back. In midair he begins to buck and twist and kick, trying to unseat his rider. I have never seen a more powerful bull in my life.

It happens so quickly that I don't even see it coming. One second the rider is on the bull, and the next he's been bucked off. I spot the danger immediately, the cowboy is hung up. His hand is caught, the bull rope still wrapped tightly around his clenched fist. The bull continues to buck, the man bouncing against his left side like a rag doll. I have to do something. Running up on the bull's right, I leap up and reach across to the man on the other side. Grabbing his arm with one of my hands, I use my other hand to untangle the rope. Suddenly the rope is loose, and the cowboy's hand is free. I let go of his arm and he lands on his feet. He runs toward the fence and climbs to safety. Slim and I are right behind him. For today at least, Bullet has lost.

By the time my dad comes to pick me up, the rodeo is over. A few people are still around, tending to the stock, but the arena lights are off and the crowds have all gone home. I'm tired but satisfied. "How did it go?" Dad asks.

"Pretty well," I tell him, "especially for my first time."

"Let's go home," he says. "You must be tired." As we walk to the truck, I ask him if we can stop and visit Charlie on the way home. "Sure," he says, "I've been wanting to see him too."

The cemetery is dark when we arrive but I've been here so often I have no trouble finding my way. I stop at a grave marked Charles Prue, 1984–2005. Bullet killed Charlie a year ago today, and there's been an empty space in our hearts ever since. "Hi Charlie," I mutter. "Whadda ya think? I kept Bullet from claiming another life today. I figure that if I work enough rodeos and do my job well, you won't have many other bull riders to keep you company up there."

Dad comes up behind me. "I miss him too," he says, "we all do. He would have been real proud of you tonight." We stand together in silence for a few minutes before heading back to the truck. And as we drive away, I'm already thinking about my next bull.

Swimming with the Dolphins

by Emma Place, age 11

LILY SAT in a deck chair on the deck of her parents' sailing ship, the *Maid of the Sea*. The sunlight sparkled on the water. It was a beautiful, sunny summer's day and they were going on a little sail in the clear, blue waters of the Atlantic Ocean offr the coast of Maine. The sails of the red boat were tightened with a loud slapping noise by a slight breeze that played across Lily's hot face. Although it was hot, the day was lovely. Not a cloud in the bright, startlingly blue sky.

Lily relaxed and leaned back against the back of the deck chair and heaved a sigh of contentment as she watched the sunlight dance across the water. She sipped her lemonade. It was not too sweet and not too sour, just as she liked it. Ice cubes floated in it and the cool liquid soothed her parched throat. Lily had long, light brown hair that she usually wore down. It created a beautiful rippling effect when she ran. Her eyes were brown as well and she was tall for eleven.

Lily's mom came onto the deck.

Emma was living in Waynesburg, Pennsylvania, when her story appeared in the May/June 2009 issue of Stone Soup.

"Lil, would you like some chocolate-chip cookies before they're gone? Your brother's hogging them down below."

William, Lily's younger brother, loved food, especially sweets such as cookies.

"No thanks. They always make me thirsty," replied Lily, taking another sip of lemonade. Talking of thirst had made her thirsty.

Her mother left as Lily leaned over the side and watched the lobster pots go by. She counted all the different combinations of colors. Pink and orange, red and yellow, the list was as endless as the sky above.

She watched as several waterbirds swam by, chattering excitedly like kids who have spotted a plate of cookies.

Suddenly a dolphin leapt out of the water in a graceful arch, his shiny gray sides glistening with the sunlight reflecting the droplets of water that poured down his curved body. He plunged back in with a splash, beak first, and was gone.

Another dolphin leapt out, followed by two more. Suddenly a pod of dolphins could be seen swimming just below the surface.

Lily stripped down to her swimsuit underneath her clothes, not taking her eyes off the group of dolphins. She wondered whether they'd swim away if she got in. They seemed friendly enough, swimming alongside the boat.

Deciding, she carefully climbed down the ladder and slid into the sun-warmed water.

At first the dolphins seemed wary, but then the first dolphin to leap came forward and nuzzled against her like a dog greeting its owner. Gradually the others came up and started nudging her as if asking her to play. She stroked their smooth skin and they seemed to like it—at least they clicked excitedly.

The first dolphin came up to her and pushed her gently with his beak as if he was asking her to do something. She stroked him, but that didn't seem to be what he wanted. He nudged her again and again. He gestured toward his back with his flipper.

"Do you want me to ride you?" asked Lily incredulously.

He continued gesturing. She gently grasped hold of his

dorsal fin. She put a little of her weight on his back. He didn't object. She put her full weight on his back and clambered on. He started swimming, his streamlined body pushing through the water. They started going faster, with Lily's hair streaming behind them. She laughed and laughed. A moment she'd never forget: riding a dolphin!

The sun looked down and shone his rays on them, dolphin and girl, racing through the waves.

Arcadia, the Adventurous Wolf Girl

by Julia Clow & Olivia Smit, age 12

Somewhere on his travels, Conroy had found it. The human pup. He had brought it home for lack of a better thing to do with it. He had thought that maybe they could use it to teach their pups to hunt, but when he got home, another thing entirely occurred...

"Conroy, Conroy! Did you bring anything good? The pups are starving and we... why what's that?" Mother Wolf asked. "What on earth did you bring a human cub for?"

She pawed it, turning it over.

"Bring it over and it can nurse with Blaze and Cassie."

"But Atalaya, I had brought it home for the pups to hunt!"

"Well, it will help us someday if we help it!"

Atalaya was a firm believer that if someone helped you, you should repay it, and vice versa. Because of this, many a time had she brought home a motherless cub and nursed it back to health.

"We'll call the human pup Arcadia, and I *will* raise it."

Julia and Olivia were living in London, Ontario, Canada, when their story appeared in the May/June 2010 issue of Stone Soup.

Conroy grumbled and growled at this, but not too loudly because mother wolves are very protective of their cubs, and although Arcadia was not a wolf, Atalaya felt very strongly about her already.

Arcadia crawled over to Atalaya, where she was nursing Blaze and Cassie, burrowed herself between them, and began to suckle. Atalaya chuckled softly and glanced over to where Conroy had stopped growling and was sleeping peacefully.

"You just wait," she said softly, so as not to wake him. "This one *will* help us, you'll see!"

She had no idea how right she was, on that warm summer evening.

Four Years Later

SIX-YEAR-OLD ARCADIA sat up quickly. What had woken her up? She looked over to Blaze and Cassie. One little tan bundle of fur told her that Blaze was still asleep, but where was Cassie? Arcadia looked all around the cave, then closer at Blaze, to be sure Cassie wasn't hiding somewhere. She wasn't. Cassie was always hiding, or playing, so Arcadia wasn't worried. She was lonely, though, so she howled the "I'm here, where are you?" howl so Cassie would come back. In almost no time she heard a rustling in the forest, but it was not Cassie who stepped out of the bushes, it was Atalaya and Conroy.

"I see you've woken up." Atalaya nuzzled her human cub.

"It's a good thing, too," Conroy added. "It's time to go to the creek."

By this time Blaze had begun to stir.

"Mamasha, Babashar," he yawned, "where's Cassie?"

If wolves could roll their eyes, Conroy would have been rolling his. He had very little patience for cubs when they weren't hunting, or sleeping. It was his turn to howl the "I'm here, where are you?" with a little more demand in it than Arcadia had used. It didn't take very long before they heard the familiar rustling in the bushes. What was unfamiliar was the low growl that accompanied the rustles. Conroy growled back, unsure of what to expect. A dark ball of fur hurtled out of the bushes and landed on Arcadia's back. Arcadia flailed her arms and legs, but to no avail. It was at times like this that she wished she weren't so different from the rest of her family. She didn't like having teeth that no one could feel when she sank them into a neck or an ear. She didn't like not being able to keep up with even Blaze, the baby of the family. And she especially didn't like how different she looked and smelled. Going to the creek was the worst, because she could see from her reflection in the water that she wasn't like any of them. She only had fur on the top of her body, and it was red, not brown, like Blaze's and Cassie's. Not even black, like Conroy's and Atalaya's. Instead, hers was red, and in her eyes, red was the ugliest color in the world.

Atalaya gently grabbed the neck ruff of Cassie (for that's who was on Arcadia's back) and pried her off Arcadia.

"Let's go to the creek now," was all she said, unruffled from Cassie's entrance.

At the creek, Arcadia was almost able to forget that she wasn't like the rest of her family. She was having too much fun splashing around with them.

ARCADIA SAT UP and stretched. After being at the creek, everyone had gotten tired and had drifted off to sleep. She had been sleeping under a large tree, in the shade, but now the sun had moved and was in her eyes. She looked around and found Blaze and Cassie just waking up and squinting because of the bright light. Blaze rolled over.

"Where are Mamasha and Babashar? They were here when we drifted off!"

"Don't worry, Blaze," said Cassie, always protective of her younger brother. "If they aren't here, then we'll just have to go look for them," and she darted towards the nearest set of trees. Before she could step into the forest, though, Atalaya and Conroy came into the clearing.

"Mamasha! Babashar!" Blaze whimpered with delight. "I was worried! I thought..." Here he broke off and looked hard at his parents. "What's wrong?" He whimpered again, this time with fear.

"Cassie, Arcadia, you come with me. Blaze, you go with Babashar." Atalaya paused.

A shot rang out, sounding much louder than it should, in the normally quiet wilderness. She and Conroy ran in opposite directions, Arcadia and Cassie following close behind Atalaya, Conroy carrying Blaze. Atalaya, Arcadia, and Cassie made it home safely, but Conroy ran for miles, with the hunter silently following. He could have gone for miles more, but he was carrying Blaze in his mouth, and that slowed him down.

When he reached a little clearing he thought would be good for defending himself and Blaze against the hunter, he turned to fight. When the man cautiously entered the clearing, Conroy threw himself on him, with all the strength he could muster. It wasn't enough. The hunter fired a shot—just one shot—and it hit home. Conroy dropped to the ground, lifeless. Blaze rushed forward, calling, "Babashar, Babashar! Get up, get up, oh please get up, there's a hunter right beside you! Please Babashar, get up, I'll be a good cub and never cause you any trouble, just please, please *PLEASE* won't you get up!" The hunter picked up the whimpering cub, wrapped it in his coat, and settled down to wait for whatever came to investigate the dead wolf's body.

MEANWHILE, ATALAYA, Cassie and Arcadia huddled in the corner of the cave. They were shaking with fear for their father and brother.

The night passed quickly but Blaze and Conroy did not come home. Atalaya finally made a decision. She told the girls to stay there while she went to look for them. Cassie begged to go, but Atalaya refused. "I can cover more ground this way." This wasn't the real reason she wouldn't let them go, though; she was afraid for their safety in the face of danger.

So she set out. She traveled many miles before she found her first clue. Smoke. The hunter had decided to make a blazing fire. As she got closer, she could hear the sound of a whimper. It was Blaze! He was trapped in a small crate lying at the feet of the hunter. But she could not see Conroy. As Atalaya looked closer, she wondered if the hunter had captured only Blaze, or if he had Conroy chained somewhere else. Only a few meters away, though, lay the outline of a wolf body. As she drew closer, Atalaya at first thought that the wolf might be sleeping, but as she came within a few inches, she smelt that he was dead. When she started nosing him, the full realization hit her.

This dead wolf was Conroy.

With a mournful howl, Atalaya threw herself at the hunter, covering the distance between the dead body of Conroy and the hunter in mere seconds. The hunter whipped around and started to reach for his gun, but he wasn't fast enough. Atalaya sank her teeth into his neck and wouldn't let go. The man sat there fighting the beast, then pulled a knife from his boot and stabbed the snarling animal in the ribs again and again. Atalaya slouched to the ground, then retreated towards home, but not making it far. A little while later she collapsed in a furry heap on the ground, never making it home.

EARLY THE NEXT MORNING, Cassie and Arcadia were playing at the mouth of the cave when they heard a sound in the bushes. They turned and saw nothing, so continued playing. At noon they were restless.

"I'm going to find Mamasha!" declared Cassie.

"Oh, don't go, I'm sure she'll be home soon," replied Arcadia calmly.

"And what if she's not here?"

"Then we'll go out and look for her."

But Atalaya did not come home, so Arcadia and Cassie set out. They had not gone far when they heard something they had never heard before. It was a roaring sound, increasing in volume as it got closer, like thunder to their ears.

Then something very large came speeding towards them, stopped, and before they could run, a man stepped out of the big, dark, noisy thing. He pointed a gun at Cassie, and then... *BAM!* Cassie slumped to the ground. Unknown to Arcadia, who thought her sister was dead, the man had used a tranquilizer on Cassie. The man walked forward, and Arcadia yelped, then retreated back to the cave.

"Wow, there really is a wolf girl," thought the man out loud, as he claimed his prize. As he picked up Cassie, he heard a low, mournful howl, like the one he had heard the morning before. Arcadia had lost everyone... her sister, her brother, her Mamasha, and her Babashar. What could she do? She was so distressed that she just lay in a heap in the corner, waiting for the light of the morning to awaken her.

The bright beams of sunlight poured down onto Arcadia's aching body. The little rock cave seemed unknown to her because there was nothing to cuddle with, no one to play with, and nothing to eat. She was completely alone and she was afraid.

She decided to follow the tracks of the large noisy thing. She traveled many miles and then she found something to eat. It was a little rat that the unknown thing had run over. She did not stop long because the little girl was anxious to find her family. A while later she finally came to the outskirts of a small village. It was getting dark so Arcadia found some comfortable bushes and lay there for the night. She awoke slightly before dawn, remembering her quest from the day before.

She promptly began circling the tiny town until she caught the scent of the "thing." Once inside the town, she began searching for the location of the "thing," and upon finding it she climbed up and began looking for her sister. She did not find Cassie, but a strange noise made her look up. It was voices of people that looked just like her! A kindergarten class was walking by in single file, and Arcadia crept up to the bushes to watch. Suddenly, she

THE STONE SOUP BOOK

heard a shrill bark from one of the tall buildings without faces peering out of the windows. She darted towards the most likely entrance—an open window—and quickly clambered inside, forgetting all about the class.

Now she looked to the most likely place Cassie would be hiding, a wooden box. She crept softly up to it and whispered, "Cassie, is that you?" But it was not Cassie's voice that greeted her, it was Blaze!

"Arcadia! You're here! He killed Babashar... and took me!"

"I know, Blaze, that's why I'm here, to rescue you and Cassie and to have my revenge."

These last words were spoken in an undertone so Blaze could not hear them.

"Blaze, is Cassie here?" she asked.

"I think so," replied Blaze. "I thought I heard them bring her in last night."

"OK," said Arcadia, "the first step is to free you."

Here she tugged, pulled, and bit at the rope tying Blaze's cage shut. Finally, it gave way. Having freed Blaze, she wandered cautiously. She could hear strange voices, but there was no barking from Cassie, and Arcadia would soon find out why. There was a sock tied around her muzzle and a long thin rope around her neck. Arcadia could see the fear and anger in Cassie's eyes. She stared in horror as two little girls were poking and hugging the frightened wolf. Arcadia could stand the suspense no longer, so she leaped into the room and yanked the cord from the surprised man. As the middle-aged woman clutched the screaming girls, Arcadia started to race out the door, when she noticed one of the girls. She looked just like her! Suddenly, Arcadia dropped the rope, and Cassie started to run away, but stopped at the expression on Arcadia's face.

Arcadia realized something that had been nagging her since seeing the kindergarten class, and the hunter's children. She knew what it was now. She was not a wolf girl. She was a human being, just like the two girls in the corner. It was then that she realized that, being a human, she would have to move away from her beloved family. The thought shocked her so thoroughly it took her breath away.

"Are you all right?" Cassie asked, concerned.

Arcadia was too stunned to answer at first, but when she got her breath back she was able to gasp out a reply.

"I just need to go back to the cave."

"Are you sure?" Cassie asked again, looking more worried than Arcadia had ever seen her.

"I just need to go back to the cave!" Arcadia repeated, louder.

"So long as you'll be OK."

"I'll be fine," Arcadia answered.

THAT NIGHT, in a dream, Arcadia was visited by the Great Mother Wolf. "You are not a wolf anymore," she told Arcadia, "you are a human. You do not belong here anymore. You must think about your future, and your family's future. What is best for you? What is best for them?" Then Arcadia woke up.

With Blaze and Cassie still sleeping, Arcadia turned the thought of living with the hunter's family over and over in her mind. She knew now that she couldn't continue living with her wolf family, no matter how much she loved them, because no matter which way she looked at it, she knew that, sooner or later, she would have to go live with humans anyway. The time had just come sooner as opposed to later. It was nearing dawn when she made her final decision. She would ask the hunter if she could live with him and his family. Having the matter settled in her mind, she cried herself to sleep.

THE NEXT MORNING, when she woke up, Arcadia couldn't stand the thought of being alone, so she woke up Cassie. Blaze she let sleep. She told Cassie that she wanted to go back to the town, and although Cassie didn't understand why, she reluctantly agreed to come.

When they reached the town, Arcadia started towards the

hunter's house, Cassie uneasily following behind. As soon as the house was in sight, Cassie visibly started slowing.

"Why did you come back here?" she asked.

Arcadia didn't answer, so Cassie didn't persist. When they got to the house, Arcadia stopped in front of the window she had entered through before, hoisted Cassie through, then climbed through herself. She started exploring, looking for the hunter. She finally narrowed all the smells down to his, inside a room with the door half open. She squeezed through, then motioned for Cassie to follow. As she did so, her tail accidentally jarred the door, making a squeaking sound. The man seated at the desk spun around. When he saw who it was, his jaw dropped.

"Why did you come back?" the confused man asked.

But Arcadia had only been taught wolf language, so the man only heard barks and growls. Arcadia felt that, as a human, she was responsible for her Babashar's death. Tears streamed down her dirty cheeks as the whole family (who was gathered in the room by this time) stared in amazement. Even though there were tears, she could still see the soft brown eyes of her sister.

"Come on!" whispered Cassie. "Aren't you coming?"

"No, I can't," sobbed Arcadia, "not after I have killed our Babashar."

"You didn't kill him," Cassie said, surprised, "that nasty man over there did."

"Well, I'm human too, so it was partly my fault."

"Oh," sighed Cassie, knowing it was no use trying to convince her stubborn sister. "I guess it's goodbye then."

"Yes, it is goodbye," answered Arcadia softly.

Then Cassie turned away with her tail dropped and walked out of the small house. Arcadia turned to the man, who looked at her compassionately, and then she slowly walked towards him.

"She needs a home," said the hunter. The wife nodded, and then the girls charged to the dirty and ragged girl. Arcadia shied at first, and then realized that the two girls were merely hugging her.

Arcadia felt loved already, so many warm faces and loving arms, she almost felt at home... the word reminded her of her Mamasha. What had become of her beloved mother? The question was answered within a few days, when Blaze, Cassie, and their Mamasha came to town. Atalaya was very much healed, and very happy but at the same time sad that her child she loved dearly was moving away. After many hugs and kisses the wolf family returned to their small cave in the forest.

Arcadia lived a long and happy life with the hunter's family. She went to school and learned to talk. Then she went to university and became a wildlife vet. This helped her family a lot and made them very happy. Her new name was Helen, but she was known to all of the wolves as Arcadia, the Adventurous Woman!

Epilogue

SOMETIMES, on warm nights, if she felt like it, Atalaya would bring Blaze and Cassie down to see Arcadia. They would never forget the human cub that brought them together again.

The Migration

by Christopher Fifty, age 11

A PACK OF FIFTEEN GEESE flew over the mainland and then out to sea. They were migrating to a warmer place. As they flew over the sea, they looked down; the sea was rough with choppy waves. The geese spotted a ship, a skipjack. It looked as though the three-man crew was catching oysters. The ship sat low in the water, obviously full of oysters.

Suddenly a strong gust of wind blew, and the geese had to adjust a few feathers. Strong gusts of wind, choppy waves—the geese were no fools, a storm was coming, a big storm at that. The geese squawked, "A huge storm is coming, we better fly faster." The skipjack started to rock back and forth. The geese heard a human shout, but they couldn't hear what he said over the wind. Suddenly another human joined the one at the wheel. The third human, the one at the oyster thongs, pulled up the thongs. The wind was blowing stronger now. The human who had just pulled up the net let the sail out.

The geese were forced on despite their curiosity. The lead

Christopher was living in Churchville, Maryland, when his story appeared in the March/April 2010 issue of Stone Soup.

goose squawked, "Move closer; it is going to get very cold very fast." The geese moved closer, so instead of a V they were in two straight lines. The brave geese flew on through the flashes of lightning, and the boom of thunder, through the insistent pelting of the rain, and the gusts of the wind. The geese were wet, tired, hungry, and annoyed. Why did the weather have to be terrible on their flight over the murky, green waters of the sea? Finally, the head goose squawked, "Almost there; I see land." The geese breathed a sigh of relief. Finally they would get a chance to dry and preen their wet feathers. They would get a chance to sleep during the migration.

A Winter Walk

by Emina S. Sonnad, age 12

IT WAS ONE of those winter days that seemed much more like spring. There had been a storm yesterday but the only trace of it now was the slightly dark mist suspended in the vast open sky. Weak sunlight crept through the open windows, casting a timid sort of light throughout the room and a quiet chirping of birds could almost be heard outside in the maple tree. It was just one of those days begging for me to go outside and find out what it would bring.

"Will someone take Scooter for a walk?" I heard Mama call. Jumping up, I skipped down the stairs two at a time, grabbing our dachshund's leash as I flew down the hallway.

"I will!" I called out loudly.

As I found our little puppy snoozing on the couch I approached him quietly, not wanting to startle him, and then whispered gently, "Hey, little guy. Do you feel like going outside with me today?" Which was of course a very unnecessary question, considering the fact that he was already starting to wake up,

Emina was living in Ojai, California, when her story appeared in the January/February 2008 issue of Stone Soup.

wagging his tail excitedly.

"I take that as a yes, then," I said happily, picking him up and burying my face in his warm fur.

Outside the weather was cold and crisp, but at the same time there was a type of warmth in the air that filled me up like a helium balloon, so that I was so full of happiness I might have lifted off of the ground. I tugged gently on the leash and then whispered softly, "Come on, little guy. Let's run!"

And with that we were off, racing against the wind that was whipping my long hair out behind me. We were racing against the sunlight that trickled towards us gently, creeping serenely into my little puppy's eyes, illuminating his look of sheer delight. It was just the perfect day to run. I looked over to my side to marvel at how Scooter's long back and powerful little legs could propel him forward so quick and gracefully. I was laughing inside, as his big, silky ears flapped like maple leaves in a windstorm. He was panting slightly, and I realized that I was too. Our breath turned into small little clouds that teased us and then floated away wispily, finally diffusing into the rest of the foggy air.

The grass beneath my shoes was crunching slightly and I was amazed at the thin layer of frost that laced every single blade of grass, big or small. I thought of how not a blade was left bare, how incredible it was that every piece was wrapped in the tiny little ice crystals.

We ran for a while, until our hearts pounded like drums. The chilly air started to sting my throat like a sharp knife piercing through my neck, down my throat, and into my heaving lungs. The dog was so swift, it was hard to keep up, but gradually his pace was slowing down. His eyes were widening in concentration as he looked up at me, signaling that our walk was now over. I nodded, unable to muster the breath required to speak, and turned towards home. One step at a time, we worked our way back to the front door. Then I turned to my beloved puppy.

"Oh Scooter, I love you so much. What would I do without you?"

My little dog's eyes dilated and he raised a paw hopefully. I put my hand out, and he jumped into my arms. I hugged him tightly and felt his soft fur against my face. Then I carried him inside the house where he knew that warmth, love, and dog biscuits would always be there for him. And he would be there, for us.

Whisper

by Dressler Parsons, age 11

CURA SMITH, a gangly girl of twelve, was exploring the desert landscape of Arizona when she heard the sound that would alter her life forever. It was the soft, normally musical mew of a cat. However, that wasn't what made Cura turn in anxiety. It was that the sound had an almost undetectable cry for help. It was in trouble.

Cura spun on her heel and ran towards the mew, kicking up dirt as she did so. Gulping, her sweaty fingers pushed back an escaped strand of ebony hair. She could feel that she was getting closer—it mewed again. Cura skidded to a stop and stepped from behind a flimsy palo verde tree. A sight met her eyes that made Cura's hair stand up on the back of her neck.

A rattlesnake lay coiled up, ready to strike. A small, cream-colored kitten was shaking with fear, his back arched. He cried once more helplessly, and the snake jolted forward warningly, then shrinking back into its coiled form almost immediately. Cura picked up a large rock and held it thoughtfully at her side.

Dressler was living in Fort McDowell, Arizona, when her story appeared in the November/December 2007 issue of Stone Soup.

THE STONE SOUP BOOK

If she hit it just right, the snake would die. But Cura wasn't stupid. She let the rock hit the ground and ran towards her house as fast as she could. The house was large, and hard to find somebody in. Surprisingly, however, her father was pacing the backyard, a tape measure outstretched. Normally he was never home, always at work at his construction business. A shovel rested in the unfinished pool against a dirt wall. Cura sprinted outside instinctively.

"Dad!" She waved her arms and ran towards him, breathless. "Dad!" Cura stopped and took a deep breath. "Rattlesnake... kitten..." she gasped. "Shovel..."

"What?" His eyes were full of concern and annoyance.

"The shovel, Dad, grab the shovel!" Cura spoke with such urgency that he grabbed the instructed object and followed her where she ran. When they got to the kitten, he furrowed his brow and turned to his daughter.

The kitten had taken it upon himself to climb the palo verde tree, and the snake was gone.

"Why did you call me over here for no reason, Cura?" he demanded, eyes fiery. Cura gulped.

"I..."

"He probably belongs to somebody, anyway!"

"But..." Cura processed his statement and let confusion cross her face. "What?"

Her father shook his head and looked at her. "Did you just call me over here to ask if you could have this kitten?" Cura's eyes grew wide, and a tear rolled down her cheek, making her freckles shiny.

"Would I do that?" she pleaded. "Dad, I'm telling you, there was this rattlesnake, and he was going to bite the kitten!"

"Don't you call me over here needlessly again, do you understand me?"

"B- But..."

"*Do you understand me?*"

Cura hung her head. "Yes, Daddy." He walked away,

muttering under his breath.

When he had completely disappeared, she gently plucked the kitten off the top of the tree and held him at arm's length from her. She looked sadly into his blue eyes and questioned him.

"I don't even like cats," she said softly. "Why do I feel inclined to help you?" The more Cura thought about putting the kitten down, however, the more her heart ached. She looked at the kitten's neck, and found it collarless. It seemed as though there was nobody to care for him.

Cura cradled the kitten in her arms and tickled his chin. He purred. "There's no reason why I can't take you home," she said thoughtfully. He wriggled, as though understanding her words. "How did you get that snake to leave, anyway? You're like the snake whisperer." Cura gasped suddenly, as a new idea occurred to her. "That could be your name—Whisper!" Whisper meowed happily. She giggled. "OK, then Whisper it is."

They trotted off for home, and Cura veered sharply to the right, ducking underneath a window. Silently she opened the window to the laundry room and jumped inside clumsily, stumbling when she landed, though managing not to make much noise. She then snuck to the stairs, tiptoeing faster than most people could run. She wasn't used to entering this way, because her parents were usually at work and there would be nobody in the house except for a fluttering note on the counter. But today was Sunday, and she had to be as inconspicuous as possible.

Where should I put Whisper? she thought. Cura hugged Whisper closer to her body and sighed in frustration. I could put him underneath my bed—no, no... I could put him in the attic—that's no good...

The door opened. Cura's mother walked inside, putting away fresh towels, and stopped curiously at the sight of Cura, wide-eyed and frightened. Her gaze traveled to Cura's arm, which was cradling a cream-colored tiny thing... which meowed. She sighed indignantly.

"Cura Harmony Smith, what do you think you're doing,

bringing that cat into the house? It probably has an owner or a disease or something..."

"We could take him to the vet," Cura suggested hopefully. "He's not clean enough to have an owner, and he has no collar." She paused and held Whisper to face her mother. He meowed again and her mother was bewitched by his big, blue eyes. "Please? Whisper was being cornered by a rattlesnake..."

"Whisper, you say?" Her mother leaned over and placed the towels on Cura's bed.

"Please, Mom. We need to help him."

"Well, maybe *you* do, but *I'm* very busy..."

"But I'll buy the food and everything..."

"Cura, I can't. I have work tomorrow..."

"Please?" Cura choked. "There's nobody to take care of him! If we don't help him, he'll die. He was given a second chance at life, and I would feel awful if we forced him to throw it away." She wiped away a tear. "Wouldn't you?"

Cura's mother bit her lip, closing her eyes as if she was pained deeply, and then slowly and softly replied, "All right."

"But..." Cura paused, and turned her hopeful eyes to her mother's. She poured a glittering smile across her tear-streaked face. "Really?"

Her mother looked away guiltily, then met Cura's smile with a half-smile of her own. "Yes," she sighed. "I... guess I *need*," she shrugged, "to help him, too." She walked over to Whisper and scratched his ears. "And how could I say no to a face like this?"

She exited the room, leaving Cura to hug Whisper once, then fall into a doze.

Just before the moon lazily drifted into the sky, fighting for admiration with the sun, Cura roused and was alarmed to find that Whisper was gone. Teary-eyed, she ran into every room in the house. Finally, she walked, defeated, into the kitchen, wiping her eyes. She saw the blurry shape of her mother pouring something into a bowl.

"M-Mom," she sobbed, "Whisper is gone, and..."

"Whisper's not gone, Cura," her mother said comfortingly. Cura curled one hand into a fist and wiped away the last of her tears, and her vision cleared.

Her mother was setting a shallow bowl of milk on the floor, and a cream-colored kitten came forward and gratefully lapped it up with his sandpaper tongue.

"Whisper!" Cura cried happily. A haunting sound met Cura's ears. The slam of the back door, the scraping of boots on the concrete. "Oh…"

"What is the meaning of this…"

"We already discussed it, honey," said her mother quietly. "We… we're going to keep the kitten." She sighed. "Whisper needs our help."

It seemed as though her father was attempting to object, but did not. He shook his head, giving in to the unseen spirit prodding him. "Fine."

At dinner, they all sat at the table and talked, which felt like a miracle to Cura. Usually, everybody would be in and out, and would grab a TV dinner when they felt like it.

"Delicious… um… mac and cheese, Mom," Cura smiled.

"It took me hours to make," she joked back, jerking her thumb happily to the empty box on the counter. Cura's dad grunted noncommittally.

"What does this cat eat, anyway?" he asked. Cura laughed.

"Cat food doesn't cost much," said Cura. "W- We could all go to the pet store on Monday."

"I have work," her mom and dad said simultaneously.

"After work?"

"How about we go next Sunday?" suggested her mother quietly. Cura gaped.

"B- But that's a whole week from now! What is he going to live on until then?" she cried. "And besides, Dad always spends all Sunday working at home."

"Work ends at a reasonable time, sweetie," her mother suggested to Cura's father timidly.

"Yeah, at five," grumbled her father. "We can go then," he continued in a warmer tone. Cura's smile was so big that she feared it would break loose.

After dinner, Cura slipped into her nightgown and pulled down an extra pillow. "Here's your bed, Whisper." Whisper trotted over and curled up, a tiny ball on the mass of red. Cura crawled into bed and pulled the covers up to her chin, then heard a noise.

The door was pushed open, and both of her parents walked in.

"Goodnight, sweetie," said her mother. She leaned down and kissed Cura on the cheek. "I love you." She exited the room, leaving an impression of warmth hanging in the room.

"Goodnight," her father grinned, kissing her forehead. Cura reached up and gave him a hug.

"I love you," she said.

"I love you too," he replied, and Cura knew he meant it. He left, turning off the light and closing the door. Whisper leapt from his bed to Cura's stomach. She pulled him close.

"Oh, Whisper," she said softly. "You darling. You're not just a snake whisperer at all," she sighed, letting him fall asleep. "You're a family whisperer."

A Calf for Christmas

by William Gwaltney, age 12

IT WAS CHRISTMAS EVE, and everything was ready. Presents had been purchased with great care months before. Yesterday they had been wrapped in dozens of pretty papers and decorated with beautiful bows. Now they sat like sparkling jewels in a pirate's treasure chest, under the fragrant boughs of a giant spruce. The farmhouse was filled with tinsel and holly and light.

The dining room table was covered with a white tablecloth, and red and green candles stood in silver candle holders waiting to be lit. Golden streams of light poured down from the dining room chandelier onto plates heaped high with frosted cookies in the shapes of snowmen and reindeer and elves. Soon these plates would need to be moved to make way for the huge Christmas Eve feast that was almost ready.

From the kitchen came the smells of cinnamon, nutmeg and vanilla, and of a golden brown turkey almost too big for the oven. On the stove, every burner was in use. Steam was pouring

William was living in Englewood, Colorado, when his story appeared in the November/December 2007 issue of Stone Soup.

out from underneath the lids on various pots, fogging up the windows in the farmhouse kitchen. The sink was filled with pots and pans and utensils, and the counters were happily cluttered. As the mother worked, chopping, stirring, and checking the pots, she sang along with the Christmas carols coming from the nearby radio.

Suddenly the door to the outside burst open and happy voices filled the air. Having finished their evening chores, the children rushed into the house, each trying to be the first to reach the Christmas cookies in the dining room. Max, thinking himself too old for such childish behavior at twelve, slowly removed his shoes and walked seriously into the kitchen. He called out to his younger sisters, "You leave those cookies alone! You'll all spoil your appetites for supper!" His mother grinned.

"Now you sound like me," she said. "Before I know it, you'll be taking over my kitchen and doing the cooking as well."

"Not a chance," replied Max. "You are the only person in the world who can make dinner smell this good." He inhaled deeply. "Did you know that it's starting to snow out there?" he asked. "There's already almost two inches on the ground." A broad smile lit his mother's face and her brown eyes twinkled.

"A white Christmas," she said happily. "It's been a long time since we've had one of those. Have you and your sisters finished your chores?" Max nodded. "Great," his mom replied, "Now where's your father?"

"He's still out in the back pasture," Max answered. "I think he's..." But before he could finish, the door to the outside once again blew open.

Into the kitchen came Max's dad, his hair wet, his clothes rumpled, and a grim look on his face. "Molly!" he called to Max's mother. "Call the vet! That cow with the white face is having trouble calving. She's been trying since early this morning, and I went out just now thinking she'd have a nice calf on the ground. But she's made no progress since I last saw her. I'm not even sure that the calf's still alive but we've got to do something."

"OK, Frank," said his wife, "I'll call the vet and be right out to help."

"Dress warmly," said her husband, "it's only twenty degrees out there and the temperature's dropping fast."

As he left the kitchen, his wife called to the children. "Max," she said, "I'm going out to help your father. I'll need you to finish dinner and feed the girls." Turning to her younger children she said, "Now, no Christmas cookies until you're done with dinner. Max is in charge and you'd better listen to him. I want you all in bed early so Santa can come. Understand?"

Three little heads nodded agreement. "Yes, Mom," they said. But as she turned around, Max was already pulling on his boots.

"Let me go out instead," he said. "You're still getting over your cold, and I'm not really great in the kitchen. Besides, the little kids are way too excited to want to listen to me tonight."

His mother smiled. "You're right, of course, but dress warmly. You don't want to get sick either."

As Max struggled into layers of warm clothing, his mother called the vet. Max headed out the door, still shrugging into his coat. Outside, it was bitterly cold. The falling snow swirled around his head. Steam rose from his nose and mouth as he breathed out warmed air into the frigid night. This was not good calving weather. The baby, if it was still alive, was liable to freeze to death before morning. The cow giving birth to him was the worst mother on the farm. She usually abandoned her calves, refusing to take care of them or even let them nurse. Now here she was having her calf in the middle of a blizzard. It was crazy.

As Max crossed the front yard, he heard the roar of an engine and looked up to see headlights coming up the driveway, illuminating the falling snow. The vet had made it in record time. Max walked over to meet him, and together they drove out into the back pasture to find his father. The site that greeted them was not a pretty one.

Max's father held one end of a rope, and the cow was on the other. The center of the rope was wrapped around a tree trunk, and his dad was trying to pull the cow up close so that she couldn't move around as much. Although she looked exhausted, the cow had the fiery glint of rage in her eyes. Her sides heaved and sweat steamed off of her. She thrashed and kicked and struggled, trying to break free of the rope.

"Hey Frank," said the veterinarian, climbing out of his truck, "she sure looks angry. How long did you say she's been trying to calve?"

"She's been at it for most of the day," Max's dad replied, "but all we've seen is one little foot."

"Not good," said the vet. "It's unlikely that the calf is even still alive. But we need to get it out one way or another. What are the chances of getting the cow into the barn?"

"Not good," said Max's father. "She's a wild one. If we loosen the ropes, she's bound to either get away or hurt us. I don't think we should chance it."

"OK," said the vet, "let's see what we can do." Speaking calmly, he approached the cow and tried to grab the small foot of her unborn baby. As the men had talked, the cow had settled down, seemingly too weak and tired to fight anymore. But now she bellowed furiously and threw all her weight to one side, ramming the vet soundly and sending him flying through the air. He landed in the cold fresh snow and rolled several feet. Struggling to his feet, he approached the cow again, limping slightly on a newly bruised leg. Her eyes rolled wildly toward him as she tucked a hind leg up near her belly, preparing to kick.

The vet grabbed some more rope and tied the cow's right rear foot up underneath her. Now she was more concerned with maintaining her balance than in fighting. "She won't try to kick me now," said the vet. "She knows she'll fall if she tries."

He approached the cow again and reached underneath her tail. Grabbing the calf's leg, he pushed it back inside the birth canal. He fumbled around for a minute, then suddenly Max saw two little legs. "I think we're OK," said the vet. "One leg was twisted backwards. I've found it now, so the baby's in a normal position to be born. The only problem is, Mom is too exhausted to push, so we're going to have to help her. I'm sorry to bother you," he said, "but I'll need a piece of rope."

Max ran for the shed, returning with the rope in hand. The vet took it and wrapped it around the calf's two front legs, which were still protruding from the cow. "OK," he said, "we're ready. We'll all need to pull on this rope if we hope to get this calf out." They grabbed hold and pulled as hard as they could, but nothing happened. Within a few minutes they were covered in sweat and gasping for breath. Disappointed, they all let go of the rope.

"Hang on," said the vet, "something's wrong." Reaching inside the cow again he said, "I'm afraid I have some more bad news. This calf is huge. His shoulders are too big to fit through the birth canal. We can either save the cow or save the calf, but you're going to have to make a decision."

"Can't we save both?" asked Max.

"There's a slight chance we might be able to," the vet answered, "but the only way to get to that calf is to do surgery on the cow. And this is not the time or the place to do that with any chance of success. It's below freezing out, it's snowing, and a pasture is far from a sterile environment. I think we need to be prepared to lose one or the other."

"I think that we should save the calf," said Max. "This cow has been a lot of trouble over the years, and the calf might turn out to be a good one."

"The problem," said his father, "is that it's unlikely that this calf is even still alive."

"Well, actually, I might have to disagree," said the vet, his hand still inside the cow. *Something* in there just started sucking on my fingers, and I believe I know what it is." He laughed. "Not only is this calf still alive, but it's hungry too!"

The vet retrieved his surgical kit from the back of his truck. Anesthetizing the cow, he made an incision along her belly. Reaching inside, he pulled out a gigantic calf. Max couldn't believe his eyes. It was the same size as a normal six-month-old calf! It was a beautiful heifer, a baby girl, with big bones and long legs. Except for some white markings on her face, she was a pretty reddish-brown, the color of henna. Her eyes were big and soft with long lashes. But she wasn't breathing.

"Hurry," said the vet. "If you want to save her, we've got to act quickly." Grabbing the calf's hind legs, the vet lifted her up as high as he could reach. The calf was now hanging upside down, but she was so long that her head and forelegs were lying on the ground. "Max," said the vet, "grab that towel. You've got to clean the mucus out of her mouth and nose!"

"Why are you holding her upside down?" asked Max as he worked.

"Because gravity is our friend," said the vet. "This will help the mucus drain out of her lungs more efficiently, making your job easier." But the calf still did not take a breath. The vet laid her down on the ground and felt for a pulse. He couldn't find one.

"I think she's gone," said Max's father, sadly. But the vet's enthusiasm knew no bounds.

"She was sucking on my fingers just minutes ago," he said. "We're not giving up! This calf has been fighting to live all day, and we're going to help her. If I could only lift her a little higher..."

Suddenly, Max had an idea. "Your pickup!" he shouted. "If you stand in the back of your pickup you can get her all the way off the ground!" The vet looked at his truck. "It just might work," he said. "Frank, can you get into the back of my truck and hold her up?" Max's dad climbed into the truck. Max and the vet passed the calf up to him. Grabbing its back legs, he reached above his head, holding the calf as high as he could. Now she dangled above the ground. Max went back to work on her nose and mouth, trying to get her to breathe. The vet began to massage her chest briskly. Every once in a while, he stopped to slap her hard.

"What are you doing?" shouted Max. "Don't hurt her!"

"I'm trying to get her heart beating," said the vet. Suddenly, the little cow coughed. She heaved a huge sigh and then blinked her big brown eyes and looked up.

"We did it!" yelled Max. "She's OK! She's going to be all right!"

"We can hope so," said the vet, "But she's not out of the woods yet. We really need to get her inside where it's warmer. Is there an empty stall in the barn?"

"Yes," said Max's dad, "but it's really not that much warmer in the barn than it is out here." The little cow struggled to stand, but the slippery snow made it impossible.

"What about the basement?" asked Max. "We've got the woodstove down there so it's nice and toasty."

"That's a great idea," said his father. "We'll put down a thick bed of hay and sawdust." Working together, the three of them carried the huge calf into the basement and bedded her down for the night. Max was exhausted, but he took the time to dry her thoroughly and give her a bottle of warm milk before he struggled back up the long basement steps.

In the kitchen, his mother bustled about, making hot chocolate and sandwiches for his father and the vet, who had just come in from tending to the mother cow. They had sewn her up and had somehow managed to get her into the barn. "It looks like she'll make it," said the vet, "but I don't think she'll be able to have any more calves." Max thought that might not be such a bad thing. She didn't seem to like being a mom much anyway.

Max's mother offered Max a mug of hot chocolate, but all he wanted was his nice soft bed. "Merry Christmas," she told him. "It's after midnight, so it's now officially Christmas Day." Max smiled and then staggered off to bed. He fell asleep immediately. In his dreams cows, beautiful cows, pulled Santa's sleigh through a snow-filled sky.

"I thought we made a deal," Max said to his sisters as they struggled to wake him up the next morning. "I'd give you one of my presents and you'd let me sleep until at least seven o'clock."

"But it's ten o'clock already," said his oldest sister. "Mom wouldn't let us wake you up any earlier. But you've got to get up. You've got to come and see what Santa brought us. It's the best present ever!" Rubbing the sleep from his eyes, Max dragged himself out of bed.

The girls tumbled down the stairs ahead of him. Then they opened the basement door. Suddenly, Max remembered the calf. He charged down the basement stairs right behind his sisters. "Look!" they shrieked. "Look! Santa brought us a new calf. And Mama said we can feed it with a bottle. And Daddy says she can stay in the basement until spring. Isn't she beautiful?" And she was.

"We decided to let you name her," they all shouted. "Dad said that it should be your job. What are you going to call her?" they asked.

"How about Eve?" said Max, as the calf sucked hungrily on his fingers. "She was born on Christmas Eve."

"Eve! Eve! Eve!" chanted his sisters. The calf bawled loudly.

Giggling, Max's littlest sister said, "I think that means she likes her new name!"

"Actually," said Max, "I think it means she's hungry. Who wants to feed her?"

"Me! Me! Me!" clamored his sisters, and they all raced upstairs to fix Eve her bottle.

A Day at the Ranch

by Caroline Thomas, age 12

IT WAS A BRIGHT and clear Monday morning on the Flying T ranch in Texas. Almost everyone at the ranch was still asleep, except a little blue heeler named Patches. She was a small dog with short brown legs and a stumpy tail. Her ears were black and she had a black patch on one eye. The rest of her strong little body was a silver-gray. She was an intelligent and spunky dog who loved to run and play. It was best to stay clear of her if you got on her bad side. Oh, and her specialty was herding the horses or anything else she thought needed herding.

SHE SAT very patiently by the door of her pen. Ears pointed and alert, listening for any sound that might signal the people in the house were up. Not very long afterward she heard the rewarding sound of footsteps. Up came the rancher; he was a tall handsome man with gray hair in his early sixties. He opened up the door to have Patches, tail wagging profusely, jump up on him as a good-morning greeting.

Caroline was living in Springfield, Virginia, when her story appeared in the September/October 2007 issue of Stone Soup.

But enough of that, thought Patches to herself, there are bigger fish to fry this morning! And away she ran on her brown little legs. First she stopped by the barbed-wire fence and barked a friendly and cheery good morning to the neighbor's dogs. When she got a mind-your-own-business bark in response, Patches trotted away. See if she ever told them hello again.

Now to the horse pastures! Patches had taken it upon herself to make sure that the horses would mind every morning. She would stealthily slip under the rust-covered iron gate and nip at all of their heels a bit before Major Ed, the rancher, opened the big gate so he could take care of them.

That always takes all the fight out of them, Patches thought happily as she finished her daily routine. It saves the people a lot of trouble too, she commended herself warmly.

Just as she was squeezing under the gate, Joan, the rancher's pretty wife that would cook tempting tantalizing things for you until the cows came home, said, "She's going to get the snot kicked out of her someday!"

Patches puffed herself up with pride. *What* a compliment! She didn't know what it meant, but it must be something good. What a compliment! She was so proud and pleased with herself that she didn't look where she was going as she made her rounds around the ranch to make sure everything was safe and normal and *SPLASH!!!!* Water went everywhere as Patches ran at a rather fast pace, into the cold pool. If there was one thing she didn't like it was being immersed in bitterly cold water. She paddled to the steps panting, thoroughly disgusted with herself and also at the cold, wet water.

Well, Patches thought sadly to herself as she drooped her head, I guess pride really does go before the fall, or the jump in my case... She stopped short though because she heard a car coming down the quarter-mile downward-sloping driveway.

She ran around to the other side of the house to investigate, coat dripping wet and gleaming in the warm September sunshine. It was an unknown car! How dare it enter her premises!

It could be a threat to her people that she had worked so hard to keep safe and happy all these years! Anger burned within her as she shook with fury and rage. She would take care of that car once and for all. Patches leaped into action as the unidentified car progressed slowly down her driveway. She ran at it with an aggressive speed, biting at the large steel-belted tires. The car slowed down almost to a stop. She was winning! Just as she thought this battle was won Major Ed came around and stared darkly at Patches, making her whimper.

"Patches! Patches, get over here! What are you doing?" he hollered.

"I'm protecting my property and you! What else would I be doing?" she barked in reply.

Before she knew what was happening she was dragged, claws dragging in the dirt, toward her pen. "Oh, no! Not that!" she begged. "I'll do anything, please don't put me in there!" Despite her pitiful cries of distress she was locked up, as the intruder stepped triumphantly out of his car and strode toward the barn.

Patches lay down her short-haired head, sighing a huge dog sigh. She had had quite a day. Why not rest for a bit? She stretched out, soaking in the golden rays that fell across her. Her eyelids drooped, almost closing, covering her brown eyes so that they could barely be seen. The next thing anyone knew the blue heeler was fast asleep, but not for long.

As soon as Patches woke up, she stretched her legs and neck and started barking. She must get out of that pen which restrained her! She needed desperately to make sure everyone was in tiptop condition. If anything had hurt them, they would have her to deal with! That is if she could escape her pen.

Her owner Brad, the rancher's grown-up son, heard her cries of desperation and frustration and came to her rescue. As soon as he had lifted the latch Patches took off running at lightning speed without even stopping to say hello or thank you. First, she ran around the main part of the yard twice to make sure everything was normal. Then, she searched the barn. There was

Major Ed and he looked just fine shoveling out the horses' stalls. Next, she sprinted over and peeked through the short wooden fence posts that surrounded the backyard. The posts were not to keep Patches out, but the housedogs in. They were worthless. All they did was bark when they felt like it and eat treats and table scraps so that they would get fat.

But not me! Patches thought. I'm very useful and needed. I make the horses behave. I make sure no snakes and other suspicious-looking creatures of the kind enter our green lovely yard. I protect my kind people and keep nasty troublemakers out of the driveway. Yes, I'm very helpful I suppose. Not saying that to be prideful or anything though, Patches thought, eyeing the sparkling clear water in the pool.

She poked her nose through the fence, sniffing the air for anything that might be a sign of danger. Nothing, she noted as she gazed at little Lexi, who was Brad's daughter, toddling around in the tall grass, followed closely by her mother's watchful eyes.

Patches turned in the opposite direction and surveyed the sprawling lawn. She determined that all was secure on the home front. By now it was getting dark, so Patches knew that it would be time to go back to her pen soon. She was getting tired too. Patches heard Major Ed coming toward her. She yawned, showing her sharp teeth. It had been a busy day! She walked willingly into her pen and lay down. As the darkness slowly settled and enveloped her she gave a good-night bark to the ranch and then fell into a heavy deep sleep.

A Hidden Love

by Alexis Colleen Hosticka, age 12

By THE TIME I was thirteen, it seemed like I was too old to admit my love of animals. I'd hidden my true feelings about the subject for so long it just didn't seem right to change them so late. When I was five, a dog had scared me badly, and for a short time I had been afraid of animals. Ever since then, my parents had been way too overprotective about keeping me away from animals, and I had gone along with the flow instead of speaking up that I wasn't frightened anymore. Now I was too nervous to tell my parents—I figured they wouldn't believe me and just think that I was saying it to make *them* feel better. But, then I met Cinnamon...

It all started one day in early August. School was going to start again in a few weeks and I was over at my friend Millaina's house.

"I'm sure that the violet dress will work fine, Millie. The color brings out your blue eyes and if you wear the little flower brooch, it'll be perfect," I said.

Alexis was living in West Chicago, Illinois, when her story appeared in the March/April 2007 issue of Stone Soup.

"Are you sure, Kirsten?" she asked me, looking at the dresses scattered across her bed.

"Yes. The green one is too bright and the pink washes you out. The rest all have their own problems. You'll look wonderful at the wedding—I promise. Can we go downstairs now?" I was getting hungry and Millie's mom always had muffins or cookies baking.

"Sure, but only for a minute, I signed up to help out at the animal shelter at 3:00 P.M. and it's already 2:40 P.M. You can come with if you want, but you don't like animals—right?" Hopping up from her bed, Millaina headed towards the stairs.

"I'll come and see what it's like, a kitten or two won't hurt me," I smiled, thinking how awesome it was that I could finally be by an animal without Mom or Dad standing there to make sure I wasn't injured by "vicious" puppies and "terrifying" kittens. Maybe, just maybe, by helping Millie out at the shelter, I could slowly show my parents that I loved animals.

After grabbing an oatmeal-raisin cookie, I followed Millie out the door and we jumped onto our bikes. The animal shelter was only a mile and a half down the road, so we didn't have to rush. We didn't talk on the way there, but I was thinking about telling my parents. I decided to keep it a secret for now and maybe have Millie come over, then have her talk about the animal shelter and... My thoughts were interrupted as Millie came to a screeching halt in front of the animal shelter.

Wiping the sweat from my brow—it was 94 degrees—I took my purple helmet off and hung it on my handlebars. Millie and I both leaned our bikes against the shaded wall and walked into the shelter. On the floor in a corner was a little beagle puppy, it was frisking around like a madman.

"Where to first?" I asked.

"I normally feed the dogs first and then the cats. But, since you're here, I can feed the dogs while you feed the cats. Things will get done faster," she said, heading towards a door marked *Food and Supplies.* I followed her and looked around in the small closet. Grabbing a bag of Andersons' Cat Food, I followed Millie back out the door. "The cat room's that way—the door says *Office*, but it's not one. Each house of three kittens gets a scoop of food and single kittens get half a scoop. Full-grown cats are all single-caged and get a full scoop." Millie headed left and I went right—to the cat room.

The door swung open easily as I pushed it with my shoulder—there was cat food in my hands. There were about thirty felines in the room, most of them kittens. As I set the bag down on the floor, I felt something rub against my sandal. Looking down I saw a dark brown kitten with bright blue eyes staring at me. I laughed and scooped up the naughty kitty. Glancing around the room, I saw that one of the cage doors had swung open. Above the door was the name Cinnamon, along with a piece of paper that said:

> Cinnamon is a female tabby. She is often escaping from her cage. No special care necessary.
> — Marie

I figured Marie was a volunteer and gently placed Cinnamon back into her cage. She mewed at me and I laughed. Latching the cage shut, I grabbed the food and, starting at the beginning of the row, fed all of the gorgeous animals. Cinnamon had the last cage and I took an extra minute to stroke her. Poor Cinnamon, I thought, I wonder who could have deserted you. She looked up and purred at me and I smiled down at her.

During the next few weeks, I helped out at the shelter many times. Each time, I cuddled Cinnamon a bit longer and stroked her a little more tenderly. I was growing to love that darling kitten.

ONCE I HAD Millaina tell my parents that I was working at the shelter with her, I planned on adopting Cinnamon. I was sure my parents wouldn't care and was looking forward to the date I planned to have Millie come over for dinner—in two weeks. But then it happened, the plan was ruined and my secret was out.

It was two days before the planned dinner and Millie and I were both working at the shelter. We were the only ones there and about to close up when a man wearing a big camera around his neck and holding a large pad of paper in his hand came rushing in the door.

"Excuse me ladies, can I speak to Mr. McLonvul?" he asked politely. Mr. McLonvul was the owner of the shelter.

"Sorry," Millie answered, "Kirsten and I are just closing up. Mr. McLonvul left about a half an hour ago. Is there anything I can do to help you?"

"Well, I'm trying to do an article to put in tomorrow's *Hilton Gazette*. By the way, the name's Mr. Clantrive. Anyway, I was wondering if I could interview you two. You know, just a few questions about the place," Mr. Clantrive asked in a rush.

Millie and I looked at each other for a moment. "Sure," I said hesitantly. "I mean, we're not experts on this place, but we know the basics and we can tell you the current animal count and stuff."

"Wonderful!" Mr. Clantrive said, taking a pencil from behind his ear. "Question one: About how many people volunteer here weekly?"

Millaina went behind the desk for a moment, fishing out the volunteer sign-up book. "Uh—this week we had fourteen volunteers, and then there are three permanent volunteers who aren't listed, so seventeen people working. There's about that many every week," she answered.

About how many cats are there currently and how many dogs?" asked Mr. Clantrive, glancing up from his notepad.

"Twenty-seven cats—mostly kittens, but there are some full-grown," I answered quickly.

"Forty-one dogs—an even mix of puppies and full-grown pooches," responded Millaina.

"I'll call Mr. McLonvul to get any more info that I need.

Thank you, girls. By the way, what are your names?" he asked, glancing up from his notes again.

"I'm Kirsten Mulgat and this is my friend Millaina Yiert. Mulgat is spelled M-U-L-G-A-T and Yiert is Y-I-E-R-T," I said, nonchalantly. As I spoke, Mr. Clantrive snapped a picture of us.

"Millaina is M-I-L-L-A-I-N-A," added Millie. If she was going to be in the paper, it was going to be spelled correctly—people were constantly misspelling her uncommon name.

"Thank you, goodbye girls," said Mr. Clantrive and left.

Millaina and I finished cleaning up the building and then locked up. We headed opposite directions towards our houses; we had ridden our bikes there as always. About halfway home, I suddenly realized that unless I could keep my parents from reading the paper the next morning, my secret would be out.

It's no use, I thought to myself. There's no way to try to have them not read the paper. They might pass the article, but I was planning on telling them soon anyway. Oh well, I guess I'll see how it goes tomorrow...

Early the next morning, my secret was no longer a secret. The article ended up being on the front page of the Neighbor section, so it wasn't something that my dad skimmed or missed. It was especially obvious that I had been there because of the large color picture below the large headline: "Hilton Animal Shelter, Still Going After 25 Years!" Apparently he had called Mr. McLonvul for more information.

"Well look at this, Madeline," Dad called to Mom.

"Why, Kirsten Mulgat! Is that you?" Mom asked, looking at a picture with Millaina and me in it.

"Yeah," I mumbled.

"I thought you didn't like animals, honey," Dad said, looking at me. "Were you just walking there with Millaina so you got in the picture or something?"

"No," I said, blushing bright red, then the entire story came spilling out.

"Well, Kirsten," said my dad, after I had completed my explanation. "I just don't understand why you were scared to tell us."

"But you're not grounding me or anything?" I asked bashfully.

Mom laughed good-naturedly, "What do you think, Shawn?" she asked, then answered the question herself. "No Kirsten. But, next time can you at least tell us that you're volunteering? Dad and I might want to come with."

I smiled, "Sure, Mom. I promise I won't keep any more secrets like this!"

The next day, Mom came to the animal shelter with Millaina and me—Dad was working. I gave her a little tour of the cat section and Millaina the dog section. Of course there were other parts of the building, but neither of us had ever worked in them. She helped out a little, but mostly just observed.

As we rode our bikes home, Mom and I talked, "You really like that little kitten, Cinnamon, don't you?" she asked me seriously.

"Yeah, she's soooooo cute and she loves me, too," I answered, trying to sound casual.

"She is a charming kitten, I like her too," Mom replied.

I looked at Mom, was she thinking the same thing as me? "Uh, Mom," I said after a few moments of hesitation. "Do you think that, well, maybe that there's any chance we could adopt Cinnamon? I mean, you just said that you liked her too so..." I trailed off.

"I was thinking the same thing Kirsten," said Mom, looking at me with a twinkle in her eye. "I'll talk to your father and if he agrees, I believe you can have a pet."

I couldn't wait for Dad to get home, though I was pretty sure his answer would be yes. Luckily, I was right.

The next day was probably the best day of my life. It didn't take long to adopt Cinnamon since the shelter already had most of the necessary adoption information from me volunteering. We stopped by a pet store on the way home to pick up food, toys, a cage, and even a little blue collar for Cinnamon. I held her the whole time, rubbing her soft fur against my cheek and scratching her gently. I had decided against changing her name, it fit her perfectly. The colors matched, and Cinnamon was full of spice and energy with a spirit of her own.

I was glad that my secret had finally come out, because if it hadn't, I would have never met Cinnamon, and without Cinnamon, life wouldn't be as good as it is now. Because now, three years later, I have Cinnamon's darling kittens; brown, little Paprika; gray, timid Ginger and courageous, snow-white Sugar.

Summer of the Sea Turtles

by William Gwaltney, age 11

THE SUN IS SETTING over the ocean as I walk out onto the porch. Reflecting the last rays of the sun, the ocean sparkles a bright, brilliant orange. I leave my beach house and walk out onto the sand, which feels cool and slightly damp beneath my bare feet. I glance up at the beautiful soft sky, reminiscent of pink lemonade, which seems to stretch out in every direction. A faint breeze sweeps in off the ocean. It ruffles my hair and tickles my face. It's the perfect night for a walk.

As I stroll down the beach, I see thousands of footprints in the sand, left over from midday beachgoers. I have never understood why everyone flocks to the beach during the daytime, when the sky is so bright that it hurts your eyes and the hot sand burns the bottoms of your feet… when the beach is crowded, noisy and stuffy. I have always found the beach to be unfriendly and unwelcoming during the day. But in the evening, the beach is soothing and peaceful. In the evening, the beach is mine. I share it only with the pelicans and seagulls, who play tag on the

William was living in Englewood, Colorado, when his story appeared in the January/February 2007 issue of Stone Soup.

gentle currents of evening wind.

The water remains warm even though the sun has almost set and the air is cooler. I walk close to the water's edge, letting the frothy waves wash over my feet. I am so lost in my thoughts, that at first I do not see the large brown mass lumbering out of the water just ahead. When I do glance up and see it, I quickly jump back in surprise. It takes a moment for me to realize that it is a turtle, a sea turtle, crawling clumsily out of water and onto land. I wonder why it would leave the water, where it moves so gracefully, for dry land where it must struggle to take every step. It drags itself determinedly across the beach, intent on some important mission all its own. I think of whales and how they sometimes beach themselves, and wonder if this turtle has a similar task in mind. I sit down on the sand to watch.

Once the turtle has chosen just the right spot, it turns around 360 degrees to make an impression in the sand. Then it begins to dig a small hole with its back feet, sending sand flying everywhere. Once it is done it seems to settle down into the hole and lies still. It happens so effortlessly that I miss the arrival of the first few eggs. By the time I realize that this turtle is nesting, there is already a small pile of ping-pong-ball-sized, leathery white eggs on the sand. The turtle continues to lay eggs for several hours. Without thinking, I begin to count. One, two, three... I stop at 100, but the turtle does not. She lays a few dozen more eggs before she is finished. When she is done she fills her nest in with sand and then, without warning, she suddenly drops to the ground. *Oomph!* She does this several more times. By the third time she drops, I realize that she is using her hard smooth underbelly to pack down the sand over her eggs. Once she finishes this, she flings sand all over the nest and the surrounding beach. Apparently, this is to confuse unwanted visitors about the location of her nest. Once she is satisfied, she begins her long slow crawl back to the ocean. Of course, as she crawls, she leaves a very distinctive track which will lead others directly to her nest no matter how hard she tries to hide it. I decide to help her.

THE STONE SOUP BOOK

Looking around, I choose landmarks that will enable me to find this spot again. Then, using the old sweatshirt I have tied around my waist, I sweep her tracks from the sand. Once I am finished, I check to make sure her nest is entirely hidden. Then I walk home along the beach, my mind still full of what I have just witnessed.

Even though I was up half the night and am more tired than I could ever have imagined, I get up the next morning before my father leaves for work. He and my mom are surprised to see me, as I usually sleep in until at least nine o'clock in the summer. I eat a bowl of cereal with my parents and my dad asks, "What are you going to do today, Sport?"

"I'm thinking of going to the beach," I tell him.

"What?" asks my dad. "I thought you hated the beach during the day."

I tell him that I am having second thoughts about that, and ask my mother if she will pack me a lunch. She looks surprised, but agrees to do it.

I have a plan. I gather two beach towels, a picnic basket, a water bottle, and my sunglasses. I put on my swimming trunks. The picnic basket is the old-fashioned kind. It is a huge wicker affair that will hold all the rest of my gear. I grab my lunch and the sunscreen my mother insists on, then head out the door, letting it slam shut behind me. I stop at the garage on my way out and look up on the shelves lining the back wall. I see an old, faded box, strewn with large cobwebs and covered by thick dust. The writing on the side of the box says *Tyler's Toys*. I open the box. Inside are things I haven't seen in ages... a ball, a frisbee, an old pull toy, and two ancient stuffed animals named Fluffy and Sticky who slept with me every night until I was seven. Underneath all this, I find what I am looking for... a plastic pail and shovel which were once a cheerful red, now bleached a putrid pink by many summers spent in the sun. I take those out and, after a little thought, add the ball to my pile of stuff as well.

I head out onto the sand and, even though it is early, several people have already staked out their part of the beach. I hurry to the area where I think the sea turtle nest is. After careful consideration of my landmarks, I am sure I have found the exact spot. I take one of the beach towels and drape it over the nest. It is an oversized one so it is big enough to cover the entire area. On the towel, I set my picnic basket, the ball, the pail and shovel. Then, for a finishing touch, I take the sandwich out of my lunch, take a couple of bites, and lay it down on top of the picnic basket. Now it looks as if someone has been here just recently and will be back at any moment. I spread my own towel close by and put on my sunglasses. I lie back and breathe evenly, pretending to be asleep, but really I am keeping a watchful eye on the nest. It is a long, hot, exhausting day. At about five o'clock, thankfully, the tourists start to leave. It is dinner time and most of them are hungry. I am hungry too, but I feel the urge to stay with the nest a bit longer. I think of all the little baby turtles growing inside and I feel scared for them. I stay until the sun sinks behind the waves, and the last of the light disappears from the sky. I head home tired, sunburned, and weary, but happy that I have done this little thing to keep my turtles safe.

I am determined to watch over the nest every day. On the second day, a woman appears. She has dark brown hair the color of coffee, and blue-green eyes the color of the sea. She's tall and tan and fit. She lays her blanket close to mine. I look up to find her watching me, a puzzled look on her face. I try to ignore her, but she shows up the next day and the one after, and the one after that. She seems to be spending more and more time studying me and the empty towel covering the nest. I am convinced that she wants to put her blanket there. I cannot let that happen.

The next morning I am on the beach even earlier. It's so early that no tourists are out yet. I must make sure that I get the exact same spot. My turtles' lives depend on it. As I walk down the beach, I see something. I am already too late. A dog is digging up the nest. I grab a piece of driftwood and run towards him, swinging my newfound weapon wildly. The dog looks up at me as I run. He has egg yolk dripping from his jaws. I charge at him and

THE STONE SOUP BOOK

swing my piece of driftwood. I miss the dog, but connect with the ground right next to him. A cloud of sand fills the air. The dog darts a short distance away, turns, and puts his head down on his front paws. He barks. The poor deluded beast thinks this is a game. My rage knows no bounds. I continue to run after him, trying to hit him, but the dog is too fast. I miss again and again as he runs in front of me up the beach. I feel a compelling urge to chase the dog and hurt him for committing this horrible crime. As I run after him yet again, a woman walks over the dunes and onto the beach. "Hey! What do you think you're doing to my dog?" she yells.

Once again rage takes the place of reason. I am furious at her for allowing this to happen. "Don't you know you're not supposed to let your dog run loose on the beach?" I scream. My face is red and my voice is angry. "There are leash laws in this town! Get your stupid mutt out of here!"

"Leash laws or not," she says, "you have no right to hurt my dog."

"If that dog comes back here," I threaten, "I'll do more than just hurt him!"

The look on her face changes then, from defiance to something like fear. I realize that she is wondering if I am crazy. She snaps a leash on her dog and, looking over her shoulder, she hurries down the beach. As she runs away, I feel ashamed. I suddenly realize that she is really just like me... trying to protect an animal she loves.

I drop the piece of driftwood and run to the nest. Luckily the dog has not uncovered very much of it. I see the eggshells from only two broken eggs. If the dog ate more, he ate them whole. I cover the nest with sand and pat it down gently. I wonder if the rest of the eggs were somehow traumatized by the dog's digging. I have to make sure that this never happens again.

That afternoon I am sitting on my towel, thinking about ways to keep the turtles safe. Suddenly, the woman who has been watching me all week approaches. "Hi," she says, "My name is

Martha. What's yours?" I tell her that I am Tyler. What I really want to tell her is to go away and leave me alone. I am wondering why she is annoying me when there is an entire beach full of other people she could talk to.

"Do you mind if I sit down?" she asks, pointing to the beach towel that is covering the nest.

"Not there," I tell her, "That's someone else's stuff. Sit here." I move over to oFFer her room on my towel.

"Oh come on," she says smiling, "I have watched you every day this week. You come every morning and lay that blanket down. You put that picnic basket on it. You put out toys. You open your lunch, take two bites out of your sandwich, and then leave it on the picnic basket. That isn't 'someone else's stuff.' It's some kind of elaborate prop. I have got to know what's going on," she laughs, "because I am going crazy trying to figure it out!"

She looks really nice when she laughs. So I tell her about the nest, and my plan to protect the turtles. She acts interested and asks a lot of questions. Once I have finished, she tells me, "Well that's some job you've been doing, Tyler. It just so happens that I'm a scientist who studies sea turtles. I'm on vacation this week, and I'm here to enjoy the beach, not to work. Still, every day that I have come to the beach, I've come early to look for tracks. I never saw any."

"That's because I covered them up," I tell her. She seems surprised.

"This means a lot to you, doesn't it?" she asks.

"It sure does," I tell her, "So please... don't tell anyone else."

"But I think I can help you," she says. "There's a local 'Turtle Watch' composed of other people who love the turtles as much as you do. I'm going to call them. They can help you protect the nest."

Things over the next few days get a lot more exciting. People come and put wire mesh over the nest. They bury the edges deep so that no dogs can dig it up. They ask me for the exact date that the eggs were laid so that they can come back right before the estimated hatch date and remove the wire. Then they mark the edges of the nest with poles and string orange tape between them. They post a sign that says that this is an endangered sea turtle nest and that there will be severe penalties for anyone who disturbs it. Then they make my day.

"We're sorry," they tell me, "but we don't have enough volunteers to keep someone on this beach. There are other beaches full of nests, and it takes all the people we have to check on those. So we're going to need you to keep doing what you've been doing. You'll need to keep a sharp eye out and tell us if there's a problem with anyone bothering the nest. Will that be a problem?" they ask.

Will that be a problem? "Not at all," I tell them. I am thrilled. I spend the rest of the summer on the beach. I get books about sea turtles at the library and read them as I keep a hawk's eye on the nest. People see the sign and stop to ask me about the turtles. I tell them all that I have learned and make sure that they are told what they can do to help. Things like keeping their dogs on leashes and turning out their outside lights if they live along the beach. Baby sea turtles crawl towards the brightest horizon after hatching. Normally, the brightest horizon is over the ocean, but artificial lights from houses and condos can confuse the baby turtles, making them go the wrong way. Then they run the risk of getting lost and starving to death, or dying of dehydration, or crossing roads and getting hit by cars. After I explain this to her, one tourist goes back to her hotel and even manages to get the hotel owners to turn off *their* outside lights.

By the time the eggs are almost ready to hatch, dozens of beachgoers are part of a huge fan club dedicated entirely to the turtles. Every day they come to the beach and look at the nest. They circulate petitions throughout the neighborhood, asking the city council to pass a resolution stating that all outside lights, even streetlights, must be turned off during turtle season. I feared that these people would only disturb the nest and its occupants, but instead they are just as interested in protecting it as I am.

Fifty-seven days after the eggs were laid, the Turtle Watch people come back and remove the wire. Fifty-nine days after the eggs were laid, the turtles hatch. We come back at dusk to find that they have broken out of the nest and are now scuttling frantically towards the ocean. A little girl walks over and picks up one of the turtles, intent on carrying it to the water's edge. "No!" I yell, "Put him down!"

She does as I ask, but says sadly, "He was having such a hard time getting to the ocean. I only wanted to help."

"If you don't let it crawl by itself," I tell her, "it won't imprint on its natal beach. If it's a girl," I continue, "she'll never find her way back here to lay her eggs." Just then, another turtle starts to crawl inland, away from the sea. I show the little girl how to bend down and gently shepherd it in the right direction.

When the last turtle is in the ocean, we all stand and watch the babies floating away on the gentle currents carrying them out to sea. I feel sad that they are leaving, yet happy that I have helped them to get this far. Perhaps in twenty years, when they are adults, some of these very same turtles will return to nest on this beach. If they come, I'll be waiting.

Greyhound Park

by Emily Ward, age 13

I CAN HEAR the crowd around me, talking amongst themselves, just waiting for the race to begin. I can hear people betting, "I'll take ten on Lightning! Twenty on Bullet!" I'm what you can consider an underdog. Lightning and Bullet, they are the true racers. I don't necessarily come in last, but I've never won.

I love the feel of racing, watching the rabbit bounding about in front of me. We know it's mechanical, but we run for the thrill of it. Suddenly, I get my confidence boost for the race. "I'll take five on Cassie!"

That's me! I think happily. *I won't let you down!* It's an honor enough to hear someone knowing my name. Usually, people refer to the lesser racers by their number. I'm number 2, I've actually grown rather fond of the number.

I can sometimes pick out individual voices in the crowd, little children talking to their friends. "I like that one the best, number 21!"

"Well, I like the black one the best."

Emily was living in Missoula, Montana, when her story appeared in the July/August 2007 issue of Stone Soup.

Suddenly a family sits down up front. Next to my pen. "Hi there," a little girl whispers to me. "Daddy, what's this doggie's name?" she asks her father.

He looks at the brochure. "Number 2... Cassie..." he mutters.

"Hi Cassie," she says. "I bet she's the best one!" the girl squeals enthusiastically. "Daddy, can we put money on her?" she asks.

The man looks down at her, and stares into her eyes for a moment. Finally, he smiles. "All right," he says softly. The man stands up. "Fifty on Cassie!" he shouts.

Fifty! Not even Lightning and Bullet get that kind of money on them!

"All right girl, give it your all," he says to me with a smile.

I prefer it on the track, I love having everyone watch me, well, watching us... It's much better than the kennel that I get forced into when I'm not out. I can't lose, if I do, then I'm gone. Someday I know I'll win. I look at the racer next to me. It's number 12, Manfred. Another underdog.

Lightning holds his head up high and gives all of us a menacing glare. Bullet paws the ground and lets out a quiet bark. I think that Bullet will win this one. Lightning strained his paw a few weeks ago and hasn't fully recovered.

Just then, the gates open. I know exactly what to do, I've done it many times before. I take off sprinting, I can hear panting behind me, there are at least ten in front of me. Slowly I pass one, I try to pace myself for the rest of the race. Suddenly I hear a noise. Faint at first, then louder, and I tune myself into it. "Go Cassie! C'mon girl!" It's the little girl from before.

With a sudden surge of confidence, I pass another racer. "Atta girl! Keep it up!" This time it is the girl's father. I pass another greyhound. Soon, their two voices mix together, into one constant cheer. I run faster, and faster. I begin to pass more and more dogs, but I don't notice, I'm listening to the sound of cheering.

Then, the noise grows, more people are standing. "Keep it up!" "Number 2 is number 1!" "Cassie! Go Cassie!" Soon I realize that I am neck and neck with Lightning. Bullet is only a few feet ahead of me. I can see the finish in the distance. Now the entire crowd is cheering me. I push myself, using the last bit of power I can muster up, I speed ahead of Lightning.

I run harder, trying hard, so hard, to reach Bullet. I can feel Lightning's dark gaze boring into the back of my head, but I don't care. Even those who didn't bet on me begin to cheer. Everyone wants to see me win, everyone wants to see an *underdog* finally take charge. Bullet shoots a nervous gaze back at me. I move my legs, pumping them faster and harder than I ever have before. I am at a dead tie with Bullet. I can hear a startled whimper escape him. He tries to push forward, but it's no use. He used all his energy with his grueling pace. I pass him, and soon I pass the finish line. The crowd erupts into one huge cheer.

"Cassie! Cassie! Cassie!" they shout my name over and over again. I've never felt so tired in my life. I pace back and forth.

I can hear the announcer, "Truly an amazing feat, number 2 has won it all!"

That night I sleep comfortably in my kennel. I can still hear our trainer's voice, "Don't know how you did it, but you did!" I can still feel the sense of importance that rushed over me as I passed the finish line. I can still see the look in Lightning's eyes. And I can still imagine the little girl, *"Go Cassie! C'mon girl!"*

My dreams of winning come to an end the next morning. I yawn, stretching my legs out as far as the kennel will allow them to move. I can hear the dogs above me shifting restlessly. I hear Lightning whimper, his paw must still hurt.

Soon, our caretaker comes in. "Hey guys. Good race yesterday, especially you, Cassie," she says and scratches me under my chin. "OK, everyone, give it your all today," she says, then she lets us out of our kennels and serves us breakfast.

News must spread pretty quickly, because today everyone is betting on me. I look around for the little girl from the other day, but I don't see her. "Twenty on Cassie!" I hear from a few feet away. I look up excitedly, but I don't see the girl, or her father. Several more people put bets on me, then the gates open. I race off again, passing others, but with no motivation for me to win. Then I see her, just behind the finish line, it's the little girl. I forget about the race, I forget about the pain in my legs, and the greyhounds around me. I run as fast and as hard as I can to get to her, and I make it.

A cheer erupts around me, but I don't care. I look around, she's gone. It was just in my imagination. "Yes sir! She's done it again! Cassie has won, with what seems like almost no effort," the announcer shouts out. I sigh, and pace back and forth. Winning isn't important anymore.

Once again, I am put back in my kennel, the rush of victory is no longer with me. I don't care about racing, I don't care about winning, I just want to see the little girl again, I just want a home...

I wake up in the middle of the night, my caretaker is opening my kennel. "All right girl, this is it. You're going to the national competition. One man in the last race runs the program, and he saw you racing. He wants you to compete," she says. I am led away from the racetrack that I have known all my life, and I am put into a strange car.

A man I don't know drives away, I soon fall asleep. I am awoken by our sudden stop. I lurch forward and almost hit the seats in front of me. The back door opens. I look out at the light. The man violently pulls me from the vehicle.

I am led into the kennels, they are slightly larger than the ones I lived in before. I am shoved into one and the door is locked. I try to fall asleep, but I am awoken only a few hours later by voices. I look up, and there she is. It's the little girl. I wag my tail and yip excitedly. She smiles and reaches down to pet me.

Her father is there also, he is talking to the man, I hear a little bit of what they are saying.

"I will pay you, how much do you want?"

"She is not for sale!"

"Please, for my daughter... it means the world to her."

"Absolutely not! The dog is running in a huge race tomorrow. And that's that!"

They want to adopt me! They want me to be their pet! I think. I paw at the door of my cage.

Her father walks over to her. "Come on Susan, we have to go now," he says sadly.

Susan. Her name is Susan. I make a mental note.

"I'll be at the race tomorrow, Cassie, I know you can win!" Susan whispers to me. Then they leave.

I sleep soundly, I can't wait to see them at the race tomorrow.

Morning comes earlier than I thought. I shiver with excitement, not about the race, though. *I wonder where they will sit...* I wonder. Moments later, the man comes in and feeds us. Then, we are led out to the track.

The first thing that I notice out there is a hole in the fence, it leads down a path, and into the forest. The second thing that I notice is Susan and her father, right next to my pen, again. "Hi Cassie! Hi girl!" Susan says excitedly. I wag my tail and paw the ground.

I hear a conversation of the two men sitting next to them. "Yeah, I'm placing my money on Cassie. If she wins this one then she's going international!" one says. Then the gates open. I run out, all of the others are bent on catching the rabbit.

Then I realize something, I'm in the lead. If I win, then I go international, and I never see Susan or her father again. If I lose, then I'm done for. I stop, and look at the others, no mind of their own. Their lives are about that rabbit, and nothing more. I was once like that, until I met Susan. Then I look at the hole in the fence. And I run through it.

I trot down the path awhile, everyone behind me is shouting, "Catch her! Catch her! She's worth tons!" "She's a born racer, we still need to breed her to get pups that are the same way!" "Quick, while she's stopped!"

I stop, and turn around. I look right at Susan and her father. I bark loudly, then wag my tail. And they smile.

Then I turn, and I do what I've been trained to do for all of my life. I run.

THE STONE SOUP BOOK